BITTERSWEET

A FORBIDDEN LOVE AFFAIR

MZ. LADY P AND CHIEF

D1607871

MZ. LADY P PRESENTS, LLC

COPYRIGHT

MONSTA

"Fuck! Fuck!" I yelled as I slammed my hands against the steering wheel.

The pain that was surfacing inside of me was starting to become unbearable. Ten minutes ago, I was pulling out of the parking lot of Magic City when a silver colored Honda Accord pulled up in front of me and cut me off.

The back door opened and a young nigga with a mask on opened fire into my Maserati. I ducked under the steering wheel and slammed the gear shift into reverse. I felt when one of the bullets hit me in my left shoulder. It burned like a motherfucker. The nigga in the back seat jumped out of the car and started bussing, sending more hot lead through my car.

Whoever this young nigga was he obviously didn't give a fuck about much and was here to body some shit. I felt a sharp cramp like pain shoot through my left leg into my toes. I fought through that shit, as my entire body felt like it was burning from within. I was losing a lot of fucking blood. I stared at the reverse screen in my dashboard as bullets continued to rip through the car. I knew once I was able to get to an open road I'll be good. After hitting a few parked cars, a wall, and a light pole, I was able to straighten the wheel and make my way

1

to Grady Hospital. I managed to grab my phone and call my right-hand man Dex, to let him know what just took place. I was trying my best not to lose consciousness.

When I made it to the hospital, I stumbled through the lobby covered in blood. Each step that I took was beyond painful. I had a medical crew running to my rescue in seconds after the front desk clerk had seen how severe my situation was. Despite being in so much pain, a woman's beautiful voice made me look around to see her face. At a time like this, I should be praying not lusting, but this woman was beyond beautiful. Watching and listening to her give orders to the crew of nurses assisting her was as bad as cocaine is for my health. She was beautiful, but the pain I felt shooting through the back of my head quickly reminded me of how fucked up I am. I reached behind my head where I felt the pain and felt my head swollen to the size of a baseball with what felt like two holes about a half of inch apart.

I was placed on a gurney and rushed to be prepped for surgery. I heard her inform the anesthesiologist that I had two bullet graze wounds to the head. I was trying my best to contain myself, but in all reality, the pain was just fucking unbearable. They were trying their best to calm me down, but the pain was causing me to go crazy.

I started getting fucking angry that they haven't given me anything yet to help with the fucking pain. I started throwing shit that was in my reach and pulling out the IV's they had hooked me up to.

"Calm down. We can't help you if you're going to behave like this. We're prepping you for surgery right now." As they tried to calm me down, I looked passed all that beautiful shit I was seeing earlier.

"Look I need some motherfucking pain medication while y'all do that shit. Fuck you mean calm down. This shit is burning like a motherfucker! I need to be put to sleep immediately!" As the rest of the staff worked on me, she walked over and grabbed my hand.

"I understand that you're in pain and we're moving as fast as we can. So far we've counted fourteen bullet holes. You've even been grazed in the head by some of the bullets. It's a miracle you're even able to talk right now. Just bear with me. I've just given you some pain meds."

Hearing how many times I had been hit up sent chills through my body. The reality of a motherfucker being brave enough to try to kill me had set in. I've been shot a couple of times before, but fourteen times and I'm still able to function is beyond a blessing. Whoever sent that hit on me will regret the day his fuck ass momma pushed him out into this world. They didn't know I was a motherfucking 'Monsta'.

SERENITY

*T*ired was an understatement for the way I was feeling. I had just pulled a damn sixteen-hour shift and had to be right back at the hospital in eight hours. As much as I want to call off, I know that I can't. I'm all about my coins, and these bills will not pay themselves. I'm trying to buy me a home and a new car outright. Besides that, I love what I do. Being a registered nurse has always been a dream of mines since I was a little girl. My mother always told me I wouldn't be shit just like my daddy. She would fuck me up whenever she caught me dreaming. That was one evil ass bitch. When they lowered her into the ground, I cried tears of happiness.

Her death is what landed me in the home of my father, Dinero "Money" Moorehead. Prior to my mother Eve's death, she had kept me from him because he didn't want her. I really didn't even know who my father was until I was about three and that was because he happened to see her ass on the corner begging for change to get high with me. He immediately took me from her. That didn't last long though because her ass called the police and said he kidnapped me. With him not being my legal guardian, he had no choice but to return me to my mom. That was the last time I saw him until I was ten when he picked me up from the police station after her death.

4

I thank God every day for my father. He instilled so much in me over the years. Most people look at my father and think of him as a "menace to society." Money is a lot of things but a menace he is not. I admit he holds court in the streets and has no problem killing a nigga that gets out of hand. I used to think my father was a successful businessman, but that all changed when I witnessed him cut one of his friend's hands off in our basement for stealing from him, not to mention finding kilos of drugs in the crawlspace of our massive home.

To the streets, he's a drug kingpin, but to me, he's just my daddy, or shall I say "My Money".

At twenty-five years old, I'm very much a daddy's girl. He still spoils me rotten, but I like to make my own money. I have my own everything because he never allowed me to just spend his money. I had to work for my allowance. Back then I didn't understand, but now I do. That's why I grind for everything that I have. I could be a weak ass bitch and depend on daddy. That's not how I roll though. I'd rather be a boss bitch and depend on myself.

* * *

"I'm so glad you're here. That nigga they brought in here a couple of nights ago has been giving me hell. I swear I'm not going back in there. He's so fucking rude and disrespectful."

"He can't be that bad, Moniece," I said as I walked inside of the nurse's station to look at my patient charts.

I was actually being funny because he was a piece of work, and I hated that I had to deal with his ignorant ass. Being that I'm her superior, I know that I couldn't let her know that.

"Well, he's on one today. Good luck, I'll see you tonight. I picked up an overnight shift." Moniece quickly left, and I got ready to do my rounds.

"Good morning, Mr. Jones. Oh my god!" I quickly covered my eyes in embarrassment.

This nigga was jacking off, and I had walked in at the moment he was erupting. That shit looked like a volcano. I was floored at its size, not to mention its width. This nigga was out in the world murdering pussy. I couldn't believe I had a damn visual of him actually fucking a bitch's brains out.

The familiar feeling in my pussy let me know I was way over due for some attention. However, I was now practicing celibacy, and I planned on keeping it that way. My ex Nas had taken a bitch through it. I was at the point where I would rather masturbate than let a nigga enter my pleasure palace. The fact that he had been stalking me didn't make the shit any better. Some days I wish that my first love Chino had never been sentenced to life in prison. Life for me would be much different. The very thought of him took me to a memory I placed in the back of my mind. Sometimes things happen in our lives that we try to act as if it never happened. Chino is one of those things.

"Come on in, beautiful. My bad. A nigga's got to do what a nigga's got to do. I've been in this bitch for damn near a week. Get that look off your face. You know this big motherfucker turned your ass on." I rolled my eyes at his ass and proceeded with taking his vitals.

"Mr. Jones I would appreciate it if you close the curtain when you want to pleasure yourself. It was disrespectful for me to walk in and see that."

"Quit fronting. I bet your pussy is wet right now." I tried my hardest not to smile, but I did.

"Mr. Jones, you're handsome and all, but you ain't all that," I said not even believing the shit I was saying myself.

He was fine as fuck, not to mention sexy as hell. When he first came into the E.R. all bloody and shot up, I couldn't really see him. Now it's a week later, and I can see him in all of his glory. Despite how sexy he is, I know that he's a gangsta. It's obvious someone wants him dead. I don't want any parts of that. I'm good on all levels when it comes to his type.

"Stop that Mr. Jones shit. It makes me sound old. I'd prefer for you to call me Monsta. That's what everybody else calls me."

He licked his lips and my knees damn near buckled. He had this cocky smirk on his face, and I wanted to knock it off. This man just knew he was the shit. I was glad I was finished with his vitals because I needed to get out of there.

"I'd rather call you Jah. You're more of a god to me than a monster." I winked at him and quickly walked out of the room.

MONSTA

I won't even front that sexy ass nurse is the type of female a nigga needs in his life. To be honest, I only started jacking my dick when I heard her voice out in the hallway. I was digging shawty from the first day I came in, and I know she don't be wearing no draws under them scrubs the way that ass be wobbling. She knows what she be doing to a nigga. I'm in this bitch full of holes and barely can move, but she still wants to be teasing a nigga and shit. The look on her face when she saw my dick was priceless. I know she's a freak hiding behind all that professional shit. Deep down I know she wants me to sink these ten inches inside that tight little pussy.

VBRR! VBBRR!

"Talk to me!"

I listened to my nigga Dex tell me that he had some valid information for me, and he was going to slide on me later. That shit had me on edge and more than ready to hear what he had for me. I knew my nigga had some feedback on who orchestrated the hit on me. I needed that information ASAP. Whoever was brave enough to make an attempt on my life should be brave enough to face his death like a man.

I started unplugging shit out of me, and the machines started going crazy. Nurse Serenity came running into the room looking crazy.

"Jah, are you out of your mind? Your wounds are not fully healed as of yet, and it's not a good idea to leave. Even if you decide to leave against what's best for you, you still have to sign off on your release papers. You're going to need your prescriptions as well. I really think you need to stop and think about what you're doing because it's not smart.

"Listen, lady, I got shit to do and lying around here fucking around with y'all ain't good for me either. Take this those are my contacts; hit me when you got my prescription. I'll meet up with you and get it, but for now, I got more important shit to do."

I walked off leaving her speechless. I was sure that she would call me later, so I wasn't worried about any infection and shit. I was more worried about getting up with my nigga and finding out who the fuck.

When I made my way down to the parking lot, I forgot them crackers impounded my car. A couple of days after being admitted, I was informed that my car needed to be taken in for investigation. I wrote it off as a loss. With all the bullet holes that were in it, I didn't want it back anyway. I looked to my right and saw a cab driver parked under the shade just chilling. I startled him when I walked up on him. I handed him a hundred dollar bill and the address to my condo downtown.

Twenty minutes later, I was typing the code into the keypad to get inside. As I walked inside, I stood in from of my huge fish tank to check on my piranhas.

It was a wonder they were still alive because they hadn't eaten in a week. I quickly headed to the kitchen to grab them a couple of fresh steaks to eat.

I jumped in the shower and got that hospital stench off of me. After getting dressed, I grabbed the keys to my Tesler and made my way to Columbus. I needed to meet up with my nigga at his car dealership.

An hour later I was pulling my car into a parking spot. While getting out of the car, I felt like one of my staples in my stomach ripped out. The shit was painful as fuck, but I popped a Perc and kept it moving. I'm glad only two bullets grazed my thigh and hip because I can't afford to be limping around and shit. It's bad enough I'm sore as hell from being hit up in my chest and shit.

I lit my Newport short cigarette and slowly made my way up the stairs. I walked in his office, and he was with a client that he quickly excused when he saw me. We gave each other a hug then I took a seat.

"Bro, the word is the old head "Dinero Money Moore" from zone six is who called the hit. He knows you were responsible for robbing and killing his lil' nigga Cameron. He gave the job to his lil' brother who just got out the state; I think the lil' nigga's name G-baby. He drives a new model Impala burgundy color. If you find him, I think he can lead you to the old man."

"So this nigga put a hit on me because one of his niggas took an L?"

"Pretty much bro, but all jokes aside you need to be careful. That old head has pull out here, feel me? He's tied in with some dangerous motherfuckers. I swear bro when I heard you took all them bullets, I thought it was over for you. All I'm saying is think about your life. Maybe you should just let that shit go, and move to a different state and start over." I looked at this nigga like he was crazy.

"Yea ight, bro! I'm gone fuck with you later, hit me if anything changes." We dapped it up and left his office.

I walked out of the office not giving a fuck about that sensitive shit he was rapping about. It's simple; a nigga tried to kill me and missed. Now it's my turn. All I know is in these streets there's rules and levels to this shit. It's killed or be killed and an eye for an eye. When I got back into my car and tried sitting down, I had to breathe for a bit. The pain that had kicked in was so intense that it gave me a headache out of this world.

I was able to get my shit together and pull off. While heading back on the highway, I started putting shit together in my head. Since that nigga wants to beef, I'm about to give him a reason to. I was just on some robbery shit, but now I'm on my take over shit. I want his fucking streets. It's time for his old ass to retire anyway.

While driving my mind ran across that pretty ass nurse. I was really hoping she called me with my prescriptions because this shit was killing me. I looked at my phone and had a missed call by everybody. I needed to rest before I start putting my plan in motion. I decided to head back to the crib with the hopes that she would call me with the prescription.

SERENITY

$\mathcal{I}$ sat on my couch with Jah's prescriptions wondering what in the hell was I doing. I had no business getting his medicine for him. Especially, when he left the hospital knowing full and well he needed to have them. I think the main reason I got them for him is because he really needed his pain medication and his antibiotics.

I had been staring at his number for the longest unsure of what to say when I called. Of course, I knew I was calling so he could get the medicine. However, I felt like this is exactly what he wanted me to do. I could tell Jah was one of those men who went after what he wanted. Nothing is wrong with that. It's just that I've never met a man who exuded so much power. The average woman wouldn't give a fuck if he passed the hell out and died, not me though. I feel like underneath all that hardcore shit there's a little boy dying to be loved. When I look into his dark brown eyes, there's a hint of mystery in them. It makes me just want to reach out and make everything okay.

I noticed that when he was in the hospital, no family members came. Only a bunch of crazy ass hood niggas would come and keep up so much shit until they had to get put out. I could tell that Jah was the boss by the way they answered to him. Everything inside of me screamed he was a thug ass nigga. I knew I had no business wanting a man like that, but what girl wouldn't want a man like her father.

I quickly shook all of the lustings out of mind and sent him a quick text.

Me: Hey Jah, It's Serenity. I have your medicine.

JAH: Bring it to my crib so you can give it to me. Just because I'm not in the hospital anymore, it doesn't mean you get to slack on your job. I'm the patient, and you're my personal nurse. Hurry your ass up. I'm in pain.

Me: Sorry Jah I'm off duty. The only reason I got your medicine is because I didn't want you to get an infection. I've had a long ass day, so you need to come and pick the shit up. Let me know when you're on your way so I can send you my address.

I was absolutely speechless at this cocky ass nigga. He was crazy as hell if he thought I was about to be his personal nurse.

* * *

BANG! BANG! BANG!

The sound of someone banging on my door caused me to jump up. I ran towards the door and peeked out of the peephole. I couldn't believe Jah was at my door. I was in shock because I never told him where the hell I stayed at. I let out a deep breath and opened the door. He bopped right past me and walked inside of the house.

"Took your ass long enough. Here's some gauze and shit to clean my wounds. Hurry up! A nigga is tired as shit."

I stood speechless watching him walk his tall ass in and remove his shirt. Some of his wounds were leaking blood, and it didn't look the good. I wanted to tell his ass to get the fuck out of my house. Instead, I walked into the bathroom and got some towels to clean his wounds.

As I stood over him, I was able to take in all of his glory. His body told a story with the many tattoos that he had on him. He was so damn handsome. His caramel tone skin looked so clean and pure. I didn't see any blemishes. His beard was long and well maintained. At that moment, I pictured riding his face like a surfboard and soaking that beard. My pussy got wet instantly. He needed to hurry up and leave so I could masturbate at the very thought of him.

MONSTA

While she was cleaning my wounds, I could tell she was puzzled at how I found out where she called home, but this is my city. Anything I need to know I will know, plain and simple.

Serenity was bad as fuck. Laying here watching her nurse me back to health started to make my dick rise to the occasion. When she saw the print of my shaft through my gray sweats, I can tell it made her nervous. She tried to hurry up due to the obvious distraction that was pulsating against my inner thigh. I could tell she wasn't ready for the type of pressure I was bringing.

"You don't have to rush baby, he has a mind of his own and to be honest can you blame him?"

"I don't know what you're talking about, but after I'm finished, you need to leave." She was trying her best not to look up at me. That only made me more attracted to her. Her reluctance was sexy as fuck.

"I doubt that you do, but I'll do that when you're finished. Tell me something, though. You have a nice place, and you're as beautiful as they come, where is your man?" *She had to have a nigga running up behind her,* I thought to myself.

"I don't have one of those!"

"Why not? You seem to be well put together."

"Because I attract niggas like you, and niggas like you are no good."

I felt a bit offended when she said niggas like me because she had life fucked up if there was another nigga like me running around town. I'm an observant man, so I paid close attention to everything she was saying to me, but when she got up and walked away, I saw how her ass wobbled in her pajama pants. I knew right there and then that I couldn't leave her crib without at least smelling that pussy. When she came back over to bandage my wounds, I slapped her on the ass. Her eyes widened, and her facial expression was so funny that I couldn't help but laugh. She looked at me in shock, as I groped myself showing her the length and width of my dick.

"You think you can handle all this dick?"

"I'm a big girl. I can handle anything. You probably don't even know how to use that thing while you're doing all of that being manish and extra."

Before I could respond with something slick, my lil' nigga Rock called, interrupting my thought process. I tried to tell him to call me back, but when he told me, he can see the mark of the beast, I already knew what he was telling me. I hung up with him and told her to hurry up because I had shit to do. Her face showed her disappointment, but work comes first. I can always come back and play with her lil' pretty ass later.

I was so caught up in my thoughts that after she wrapped my shoulder, I quickly grabbed my shit and left. When I got to my Porsche, I checked for my .45, but quickly remembered I left it under her sofa, damn. By the time I was walking back to her house, she was already on her way to me with it wrapped in a towel. She handed it to me and shook her head.

"You need to be careful, Jah. I don't want to see you back in the E.R."

Instead of responding, I jumped in my truck and cruised up to the exit to get on the highway. I needed to get to lil' homie to see if what he is seeing was accurate, but the entire drive I couldn't shake her fine ass out of my mind. To be honest, a bitch is the last thing on my mind.

Bitches are a distraction, and with what I got going on right now, I need to stay focused.

Women want three things from a nigga— money, dick, and obedience from a nigga. I got the money and definitely the dick, but I'm unruly. That's where I always get in trouble with these females. Instead of playing myself and getting into relationships, I fuck and keep it moving. Honestly, to me, relationships are for suckas. A nigga like me can't and wouldn't ever be locked down by a bitch— that's against my DNA, straight up.

When I pulled into my lil' nigga's garage, he quickly opened the side door for me. He led me into the basement and showed me the nigga they had hog tied on the floor.

"This is one of the niggas that was a part of the hit on you."

"Is that right?"

I took my jacket off and walked around the nigga who had pissed and shitted on himself. The tears that streamed down his face told me all I needed to know about him. He was a pussy nigga. There was no need for me to try and make him beg for his life. That shit needed to be ended immediately. He was a coward, and he had no heart. He was walking around here doing hits but can't handle that pressure when it's time to pay the piper.

"What you want to do with this nigga? He's stankin' like a motherfucker."

"Plug that saw up for me."

I needed to make this shit quick and painful for him. He was already a bloody mess from the beating my young nigga had put on him. Once he plugged the electric saw up, he handed it to me. Without hesitation, I cut the niggas head off and placed it inside of a box. I took the box and delivered it to one of Money's blocks. I made sure to leave them a message that I stuffed inside the mouth of the head. *You niggas deliver shots I deliver heads!*

These niggas had no clue that they were really dealing with Monsta.

SERENITY

$\mathcal{I}$ was so disappointed in Jah when I noticed that he had dropped his gun. The fact that he even had that shit on him spoke volumes. It didn't matter how attracted I was to him. That hardcore shit was a turn-off. I think my problem with dealing with him is fear of the unknown. I just know the life he's living will only end up with him being locked up or in the damn morgue. I just keep seeing him coming through the emergency room all shot up.

It was so crazy how after I had handed him his gun I stood watching him drive away. His music was so fucking loud that I could hear him a mile away. I was trying my best not to think of him, but it was hard as fuck. Just the thought of him made my pussy wet as fuck. I was mad as hell just thinking about how I showed the nigga my hand when he was stroking his dick. Jah really thought he had me where he wanted, enticing me with that big motherfucker. Just the thought of how big his dick was had me having flashbacks. The feeling in my pussy was nothing but a reminder of how long it had been since I had sex.

I'm actually glad he had to leave because I was about ten seconds from throwing that celibacy shit out the window. The more I think about it, the more I'm convinced that I need to stay clear of Jah. It doesn't matter how fine or sexy he is. Jah is a heartbreaker, and I'm not trying to get my heart broke behind his thuggish ass.

* * *

"WHAT'S UP, STRANGER?" my father said as he kissed me on the forehead.

"Don't do me like that, Daddy. You know I'm busy with work." It had been a minute since I had come to visit my father. I was now feeling bad because I could tell he missed me.

"Your ass is going to make me force you to move back home. You should never go more than a couple of days without checking in. I know that you're grown and want your independence, but I be worried about you. Keep in touch more often. Now tell me what's been going on with Nassir."

I rolled my eyes at the mention of his fucking name. I swear I hated Nas more and more as the days went by, especially since he's been calling and threatening me. I had to block him from all of my social media accounts and from calling my phone.

"Nothing is going on. I'm not dealing with Nas anymore, Daddy. I'm tired of him and his whorish ways. Every time I turn around I'm finding out about him and some chick. I'm good with the single life right now, but enough about me. What's going on with you and Keelah?" I smiled, asking my daddy about his much younger girlfriend.

One would think I would be upset that my dad fucked with a girl my age, but I wasn't. I loved me some Keelah, mainly because I know that she loves my father for him and not for his money or status. The only problem was that my father was a ladies man and he needed a different flavor every day of the week.

"She's gone on vacation to the Dominican Republic with her friends. Kee-Baby is mad at me right now. To get back in her good graces, I had to spend some bands on her and send her on an extended vacation until she gets her mind right. You know Kee-Baby is spoiled and when she doesn't get her way she tends to get crazy. I couldn't have that shit while I got this beef going on in the streets."

I looked surprised hearing my father say he had beef. Things had been quiet these last couple of years. So, I was shocked to hear him say that.

"Don't worry about it. It's just some little nigga thinking shit sweet. I want you to watch your surroundings and be careful at all times. As a matter of fact, I'm going to put some of my men on you. I really wish you would move back home so that I could keep a good eye on you. I be worried about you living all by yourself."

"No, Daddy. I don't want anyone following me around. I keep my gun on me at all times. Although I hate guns, I have no problem with my trigger finger when it's needed. Be careful, Daddy. You're getting too old to be out in the streets having beef. You should be in the Dominican Republic with Keelah. Love you, Daddy. I have to go. I'll make sure to check in every day."

I kissed him on the jaw and rushed out of the house. I knew that he was about to give me a lecture about being safe and I didn't have time for it. Plus, I had called off from work. I just wanted a day just to relax and pamper myself.

After several hours of sitting in the hair and nail salon, I was dog ass tired. I had plans on meeting up with Moniece later for drinks. I was in need of a power nap. When I pulled into my driveway, I was ready to snap. This nigga Nas was sitting on the hood of his car blasting music.

"What the fuck are you doing here? Cut that shit down before you get me put out." I went inside my trunk and grabbed my bags before headed up to my door.

"Why the fuck are you not answering the phone for me? I've been calling you and messaging you like crazy. What the fuck is wrong with you?"

"Look, Nas, I told you I couldn't do this anymore. I'm quite sure there's a bitch out there waiting on you to wife them up. I simply can't take you continuously cheating and thinking that shit is okay. Please leave my house, Nas."

I turned to go inside, but he grabbed me by the back of my neck. He forcefully smashed my face into the wall.

"Fuck you mean we done? Bitch, we not done until I say we're done."

"Get your fucking hands off of me." I started swinging on his ass, but I wasn't no match for him. He drew his hand back and slapped me. I was literally in shock because that slap stunned the fuck out of me.

"Stop fucking playing with me, Serenity. When I call your fucking phone, you need to answer it. When I come over here, your stanking ass had better welcome a nigga with open arms. I hope you don't call yourself fuckin' with any of these lame ass niggas because I will kill their ass and you too."

Nas walked out of the door and slammed it. I jumped up, locked all of the doors, and put on the alarm system. I could tell shit was going to get serious with this nigga. He couldn't take no for an answer, and I knew if I told my daddy he was going to murder Nas' ass. I didn't want his blood on my hands, but him putting his hands on me was a no-no. At the same time, I knew I had to tell my daddy because this nigga was out of his mind thinking he was going to just show up at my house when he felt like it. Nas definitely did not want the problems that came behind fucking with me.

* * *

AFTER TAKING A LONG NAP, I woke up and got prepared to go out with Moniece. I looked in the mirror, and I instantly became heated. I had a big ass bruise on my face. For a minute I wanted just to call Moniece and back out, but quickly decided against it. It had been a minute since I went out. I put some concealer on my face and got dressed.

About an hour later I arrived at the club. I wasn't surprised that Moniece hadn't made it yet. That bitch is always late, even for her damn shifts. I decided to sit at the bar and order me a drink. Before I could even call for the bartender, there was a lot of commotion going on. I looked over to one of the VIP sections and noticed it was Jah and his crew. It looked like they were celebrating someone's birthday. I quickly turned around and tried not to be noticed.

"Excuse me, my boss is asking for your presence in his section." I turned around and a big ass Debo looking nigga was damn near grabbing me out of my seat.

"Who in the hell is your boss?" I asked as I yanked away from his ass.

He turned around and looked at the section. I followed his eyes with mine, and they laid on Jah staring at me intensely as he turned up a bottle of Remy. I slowly got up from the bar and slowly walked over to the section. I rolled my eyes as I entered the section. It was full of niggas and naked ass bitches. These hoes all looked thirsty as fuck.

"Get off that jealous shit," Jah spoke deeply into my ears.

I just shook my head at his cocky ass. I didn't have shit to be jealous about. Even with my clothes on, I looked better than these hoes. Not to mention the fact that this nigga is not even my man.

"Shout out to that nigga, Monsta! It's a real nigga birthday. Happy Birthday, my nigga! Keep them bottles and bitches going to his section.

The club just started going wild for him. He just sat stoic holding his glass in the air quietly thanking everybody. I was about to go sit next to him, but he grabbed a big booty bitch and pulled her on his lap. She started giving him a lap dance, and he was making it rain money all over her. A text from Moniece came through my phone letting me know she was here. I left the section without saying shit to Jah. Fuck he wants me in his section for. Fuck him and his birthday.

MONSTA

I looked on as Serenity walked away disappointed that I reached for another woman to entertain. I was digging her, but I didn't have to explain my reasons to her at least not right there and then. There wasn't no denying her beauty and the air of surety that surrounds her.

Because I was into her, was why I protected her. Ain't no telling who was in the club and who was watching, and these niggas ain't playing fair out here. They would hurt the things you love to get to you and to prevent that, I had to play her in front of everyone.

Moments later a small crowd started to form over at the bar, I stood to my feet to make sure it wasn't a distraction in all reality it could be a hit. I really wasn't supposed to be doing no wild shit like this. It's beef out here in these streets, and I'm partying like shit ain't real right now. Shit! It's was my dirty thirty birthday bash, and I was going to party like it was my last day on Earth.

As I look on at the commotion, I realized that it was some nigga standing in front of Serenity. He was all in her face, and I could tell she was scared. The nigga all the way in violation for one, because it's my birthday, and for two he disrespecting what's mines. Yeah, I know we ain't official, but I stake claim to what the fuck I want. The moment he put his hands on her was when my niggas moved in with the quickness. Dude ain't even see it coming when my lil' niggas Duke and Bruno snatched his dumb ass up.

"Take that nigga to the garage and make sure Serenity gets home safe." I continued to enjoy my party and prepare myself to fuck this nigga up afterwards.

* * *

I MADE my way to the garage of Duke's granddaddy up in Decatur. Dude was tied to a chair and gagged. He was knocked out cold. I reached back and slapped the shit out of this fool, and he was still dead to the business he was about to get into. I reached for the hammer, and with all my might I brought it down on his knee cap hearing bones crack and him gasping back to reality.

His screams were muffled by the rag that was taped to his mouth. He started looking around the room with obvious horror in his eyes. He should be fucking worried at this point. This shit always amazes me and disappoints me at the same time. The fact that niggas be all tough and brave up until that point when a real street nigga applies that pressure.

This is the same nigga that just laid hands on a female, but now he's hollering like a bitch over a broken ass kneecap. This is so sad if only Serenity could see the weak ass nigga she had hitting on her. I haven't even started yet, and this nigga crying and some more shit.

"I see you have a problem with keeping your hands to yourself, but I'm going to fix that for you."

I grabbed a pair of garden shears and started cutting his fingers off one by one. For some reason, torturing a motherfucker gave me the best hard on in the world. Not even a bitch's sweet pussy could satisfy me more than seeing the fear in a nigga's eyes before I end his life. After cutting off his fingers, I cut the ties off of him that held his arms behind his back.

"Hold his bitch ass down!" He was starting to get buck and try to get out of my grasp, but I was nowhere near done torturing his bitch ass. I started cutting his ligaments off one by one. Before the nigga died, I took a sharpie and wrote *I'm sorry I put my hands on you* across his chest.

I had my niggas drop what was left of him off in front of the hospital where she worked. I tried calling Serenity, but she sent me straight to the voice mail. I know she was upset about me pulling that stripper on my lap in front of her, but in time she will see nothing is ever what it seems.

* * *

"WHAT ARE YOU DOING HERE?"

"What does it looks like I'm doing? I'm cooking you breakfast."

"Yea! You broke into my home, and now you're in my kitchen butt naked cooking me breakfast are you kidding me?" Serenity was standing in the doorway of the kitchen with her hands on her hips looking sexy with a mean ass mug on her face.

"Calm down. Why haven't you been answering my calls or texts?"

I knew she called herself trying to teach me a lesson, but I needed her to know the method to my madness. The way I moved was only a gesture of my protection. I'm digging her, and she needs to shut the fuck up and let me run shit right now. Instead of going back and forth with her, I grabbed her by her arms and sat her down. I wanted to try and explain to her my actions, but she was just too damn emotional for me.

"Please, Jah! Just go. I don't have time for this. Go on back to the club with them bitches. You're just full of games. I'm good."

"Nah! You're not good but let me make you great."

I wrapped my hand around her throat and with the other firmly gripped her ass. She gasped as I slipped my tongue inside of her mouth and forced a passionate kiss. I turned her around aggressively, pulled her skirt up, and pulled her white cotton panties to the side. I grabbed a fist full of her hair as I slapped her fat ass cheeks. Serenity began to squirm in pleasure. I squatted behind her blinking twat and watched as her juices begin to leak. Her clit was stiff and protruding, so I sniffed her deep and hard, so the air from my nostrils would tickle her most delicate areas. She jumped so far forward from me that I had to hold her with all my might. She wasn't about to talk all that shit and not be able to take me licking on that pussy. My tongue is deadlier than my dick. I have the power to make a bitch speak in tongues with my tongue game alone.

SERENITY

y eyes rolled in the back of my head as Jah ate my pussy. I felt like I was having an outer body experience. I had my pussy ate before but nothing like this. I gripped the sides of the counter because I felt like I was going to lose my balance at any moment. This nigga was a beast with his tongue game. I closed my eyes and bit my bottom lip. I felt him inserting his fingers inside of my pussy as he continued to eat the shit out of my pussy. This nigga was eating my pussy like he was a pussy connoisseur. This nigga knew his way around the pussy believe that shit.

"Mmmmmm! Oh shit, Jah! I'm about to cummmmm!" He quickly stopped and began to fuck me roughly with his fingers.

"Yeah, that's right! Make that pussy come for a real nigga." He had curved his fingers inside of my pussy, and they were hitting a spot I never knew existed.

"What are you doing to me?" I moaned out.

"Everything that the other nigga never did." The sound of his deep masculine voice in my ear caused me to erupt like a volcano.

"Ahhhhhh!"

"Yeahhhh! That's right make that pussy squirt."

As he spoke, my juices continued to flow down my legs and form

MZ. LADY P AND CHIEF

into a puddle on the floor beneath me. My legs felt like noodles as I tried to stand on my feet. Jah quickly spun me around and kissed me deeply. The scent of my pussy invaded my nostrils. Never in my life had I tasted something so sweet. I know it sounds weird, but that's just the way I felt about it. I pulled him in closer, but he quickly pulled back. I went to grab his dick, and he knocked my hand away.

"Why are you pushing me away?"

"I'm not pushing you away. I had to fuck your mind first. Next time around, I'll fuck your body so that I can own your soul later. Eat your breakfast it's the most important meal of the day."

He kissed me on the forehead and walked to the back of the house. I couldn't help but look at his nice firm ass. I wanted to smack it, but I knew niggas didn't like gay shit like that. Jah had me so fucked up in the head that I couldn't even eat the food he had cooked. I swear this man had me confused as hell. I come home, and he's naked cooking. He ate the fuck out of my pussy but was not trying to give me the dick. That's what the fuck I really want. Now he got me feening to feel him inside of me. I swear he was so full of mind games. About ten minutes of sitting in deep thought, I felt Jah's presence behind me. Before I could say anything, he cut me off.

"Don't go to work today. Stay home and relax." He moved a piece of hair from my face and lifted it up so he could look directly into my eyes.

"I can't afford to miss work Jah."

"I said stay home. I'll pay you for the day."

He placed another kissed on my forehead and headed out of the door. I didn't know what the hell this nigga had going on, but I was confused to the point where I needed to talk to someone. I couldn't talk to Moniece because I knew that she would judge me. From the jump, she's been telling me to leave him alone. I most definitely couldn't talk to my daddy. So that left Keelah. I knew I could tell her anything and she would never tell my daddy.

* * *

"WHAT'S UP? I haven't talked to you in forever," I said as I walked inside of Keelah's Beauty Salon. Keelah was one of the coldest beauticians in the South. She was sought after, all over. She became famous off of her many IG photos of slayed hair do's. She had become a traveling hair stylist to some of the hottest celebrities.

"I've been on vacation. I just came back a couple of days ago. Your crazy ass daddy has been holding me hostage since the plane landed."

"Where's he at anyway?"

"He had to take a flight this morning out to Chicago. He needed to meet with some of his associates out there. He told me he didn't know when he was coming back. That ain't shit but an excuse to fuck with that bitch Jai. I swear to God if I have to catch a flight to the Chi it's going be more than bullets flying over there. I'm seriously tired of him thinking he slick. His old ass gone catch a heart attack trying to fuck all these different bitches all the time."

I just shook my head because all they did was argue and fight. She catches him cheating, and he cashes out on her— end of story. I really don't understand why she's showing out. Keelah knows damn well she ain't gone do shit or leave, so I don't know why she's fronting.

"Y'all are crazy."

"That's your daddy. Any who, what brings my favorite girl this way? Your sew-in is still looking good, so I know you're not here to get your hair done. What's going on? I have some time to talk before my next client arrives." Keelah gestured for me to head back to her office and I followed her.

"I'm so messed up in the head behind this nigga named Jah."

"Oh shit! Spill all the tea. It's about time you're giving that pussy up to someone else. I can't stand that fuck nigga Nas."

"See that's the thing. We haven't had sex yet. It's like he's mentally preparing me for sex with him. He's like nothing I've never met before. A couple of weeks ago he came into the hospital all shot up, and I was his nurse. I don't know what it was I just became instantly attracted to him. I swear my pussy literally gets wet thinking of him. Once he left the hospital, I have seen him a couple of times. I mean he's even been over to my house.

This morning I come home from work, and he's butt naked cooking me breakfast. Now normally I would be like I have a stalker on my hands, but seeing his body in all its glory had me wanting to suck that nigga dick like a strawberry Charm's sucker right there. Girl, one thing led to another, and he had a bitch bent over the counter eating my pussy like it was the Last Supper. That nigga made me squirt, and I ain't ever done that shit before. I was ready to fuck right there on the kitchen floor, but this nigga stopped and put his clothes on. He said he wanted to fuck my mind first, then my body, so he could take my soul."

"Dammmnnnn Serenity! That nigga's a savage. You got to be careful. You're not fucking with no rookie. That nigga is either the truth or a motherfucking con artist. Either way, he sounds like he got that type of dick that will have a bitch in the corner pulling out her fucking hair. The look on your face lets me know he's already got your mind. Make sure you let me know when he gets that body, bitch." She laughed.

"So, what do you think I should do. He's like nothing I've ever experienced before. On the one hand he comes off as crazy, and I want to stop fucking with him, but on the other hand, it's like what do I have to lose. I want to live a little. I can tell fucking with him will be an adventure."

"I say go for it. You only live once. Let that nigga knock the dust off that pussy. Just don't tell your daddy I'm encouraging you. He will kick my ass."

"Trust me; I'm not telling my daddy shit about me even entertaining anyone." The sound of my phone alerting me that I had a message made me grab my phone from my clutch purse.

Moniece: Bitch! Why you didn't come to work. The damn news people have been here all damn day. Apparently, someone tortured some nigga and dropped his body off at the hospital emergency entrance. Here's the kicker. Whoever did this to the nigga carved the words "He'll never hurt you again" across the damn torso. Guess who that nigga was.

Me: Girl who?

Moniece: Nas! Bitch, call me. Don't tell nobody what I just told you tho. I had to take a deceased patient to the morgue, and that's how I was able to see. His ass didn't have a head, but all of his credentials were sitting on the desk.

I dropped my phone so hard that the damn scream cracked. It was all coming to me now. Jah had killed Nas for slapping me. That's why he was at my damn house and wanted me to stay home from work.

"I-I got to go Kee-Baby! I'll call you later."

I kissed her on the jaw and rushed out of the shop. I did way past the speed limit getting home. I was scared shitless. When I made it home, I called Jah over and over, but he never answered for me.

MONSTA

The same day I got out of the hospital, I placed word throughout the entire east and west side of Atlanta. I had ten bands on the head for the whereabouts of the lil' nigga G-baby. This morning while I was watching the local news go crazy about the work we put in on that fuck nigga Nas. I got an anonymous text message telling me that they got the information I was looking for. They wanted me to meet them at Lavish Bistro on Covington Highway that night. I arrived around twelve, and because I knew the head of security, I was able to park my 2017 Denali upfront without having to pay a dime.

I got out the truck and showed love to the lil' niggas who looked up to me. A lot of them seemed to be amazed that they were in my presence while the others who saw me as a challenge looked on in pure envy and amazement. These niggas were probably baffled that I'm still alive. I was leaning against the hood of my truck talking to my lil' partner Mark when a white Nissan Altima pulled in right beside me. There was a black ass nigga driving looking like a base head. The woman who was on the driver side with the scarf on her head got out of the passenger side and walked up to me.

"Hey, Monsta. My name is Janet, and I have some information that can help you." Before she could finish, I quickly silenced her. I didn't need all of these niggas knowing what the hell she was about to say.

"Hop in my truck, and we can finish talking. Mark, keep an eye open for me while I holla at her."

I hopped inside and made sure that Mark was in close proximity just in case some shit kicked off while I was seeing exactly what she had to tell me. I flamed up a blunt and gestured for her to start talking.

"A couple of weeks ago I watched G-baby kick my husband's teeth out of his mouth because he owed him one hundred dollars. He and his brothers beat him so bad that he's still in the hospital in a coma. He has swelling on his brain, and there's a chance when he wakes up he won't be his old self. I had been hearing in the streets about you looking for him, so I decided to come and tell you what I know instead of them damn crackers. Now I'm not going to pull your leg and bullshit you. I don't know his exact whereabouts, but I do know where his mother stays. He and his brothers love their mother, so I know he's been to see her. I'm going to give you his mother's address, and I guarantee you'll find what you're looking for. I pray you find that little motherfucker. My husband didn't deserve that shit. I swear this shit has made me want to stop getting high and get my life together."

"Put the information in here."

I was happy as hell I at least had a location of where I could find this lil' nigga at. When she was finished, I reached inside my console and gave her some money for her troubles. Her eyes lit up like a Christmas tree seeing the money. All that rehab shit went out of the window.

* * *

I WASTED no time on the information given to me because in times of war every second is vital. I had my nigga Dex meet me down the street from the nigga's momma house. It was located in one of those cookie cutter neighborhoods off on Bouldercrest. Dex picked me up in a bakery van he stole a few blocks up the street. It was three in the morning, so we were expecting ninety percent of the neighborhood to be asleep. When we got up to the address, we were swift and precise not wanting to alarm any nosy neighbors or startle anyone that may be on the inside.

I sprayed Nitro on the door handle and waited fifteen seconds before knocking it off. Once on the inside, it was evident due to the pictures along the walls that we were in the right house. I heard some snoring, so I made my way to where the sound got closer. When I pushed the door open a woman was laid out in bed fast asleep. Her mouth was open, and she lay naked with her huge tits hanging on both sides of her.

I stepped closer inside the room and realized there was a nigga under the cover beside her. I signaled for Dex to clear the rest of the house while I got the dosage ready for both of their ass. I heard Dex whispering to get my attention when I look up he pointed to the room he was standing by. I walked over to see what had him going crazy. Then when I looked into the room, it was a baby boy. He had to be around four or five years old.

I didn't give a fuck he was coming with us. Plus he looked like them niggas. He was probably one of their sons. Fuck him! He might grow up seeking revenge, and I don't got time for it.

I injected all three of them motherfuckers with a light dose of anesthesia. After waiting about thirty minutes to make sure the shit took effect, we hauled them out of the house and into the van. We drove up to Camp Creek and found a spot in the woods that a train frequently rode through. I had already timed the trains run times and knew that the next one would be coming in forty-five minutes.

I had Dex bring them out of the van while I tied all three of them on the train track. As I tied the little boy, I decided to spare him and sit him off to the side. Killing the woman and man alone was more than enough to send a motherfucking message. After carefully making sure we didn't leave any evidence behind, we set off in the distance and waited until we heard the roaring sound of the train coming.

SERENITY

*I*t's been about three weeks since I last saw or spoke to Jah. The fact that he wasn't answering his phone was pissing me off. I know for a fact he had seen me calling him. He was leaving my messages on seen and not responding. That shit was burning me up. I hated the type of power he was having over me. It's like I can't get him off of my mind since our encounter at my house, not to mention the fact that I know he killed Nas. That's another thing that's been bothering me. In a way, I feel responsible for his death. He put his hands on me, and Jah fucked that nigga up. I'm not going to front or lie. That shit turned me on. I guess that's why I'm walking around this bitch smoking blunt after blunt.

"I can't believe you really like him? He's rude and arrogant as fuck," Moniece said. We were both in the parking lot talking after our shift was over.

"I know. He's both of those things, but it's something deeper within him that turns me on or has me in awe of him. It's hard to explain."

"Does your father know about him?"

"Are you crazy? Hell no! My daddy would kill me if he found out I was fucking with some street nigga like Jah. Plus, you know that he wants me to be with Nas."

"Well, we both know that will never happen. Nas ass is swimming with the fishes courtesy of your psycho ass boo. Let me get my ass home; I have to be right back here at seven." We hugged and parted ways.

About an hour later, I was home and bored as ever. Since I was off, I decided to get dressed and go to Jay's Lounge. The biggest all white party of the year they had been advertising on the radio. Not to mention flyers were everywhere. It was imperative I got out of the house for a change. I needed to do something to get my mind off of Jah's ass. I rolled me a fat ass blunt and poured me a glass of Remy. I got tipsy as I got dressed. I was feeling pretty damn good when I made it to the party, not to mention looking sexy as hell. I was rocking an all white one piece body suit with a pair of studded red bottoms.

It was packed to capacity, and I could see that the whole damn city of Atlanta was in attendance. I immediately became uneasy. I've never been one to like crowds. I damn near wanted to turn around and go back home, but I was looking too fucking good for that. I grabbed me an empty seat at the bar.

"Can I get you something, beautiful?"

"Remy and Red Bull."

As I waited for the bartender to bring my drink, I scanned the room. For a minute I thought my eyes were deceiving me. It was crowded, so I had to stand up and look through the crowd. All I could do is shake my head as I observed Jah headed to VIP with his usual entourage. He looked good in his all white linen suit and Salvatore Ferragamo loafers. His ice was shining under the bright lights. I hate to admit it, but that nigga cleaned up nice as hell.

The bartender sat my drink down, and I paid her for it. Instead of storming over to where he was at, I decided to fall back and peep the scene.

As I sipped my drink, I observed him in his element. It was such a turn on seeing him own the room. It's like niggas broke their necks to respect and bitches broke their necks to get close to him. The

36

numerous amounts of bottles that were being sent to his table only made him and his crew get louder and rambunctious.

I decided to see if he would answer my call. I pulled out my phone and called him. In the distance, I could see that he looked at the screen and denied my call. That shit had me livid, and I couldn't sit in my seat a moment longer. I knocked the rest of my drink back, and I made my way over to his section.

"So, this how you're doing it, Jah?"

He was seated, and a bird ass bitch was sitting his lap. Had I been thinking logically I would've just taken it as my cue to walk away. However, I had liquid courage, so all logic went out of the window as I stood in front of him.

"What's good, ma?" he asked nonchalantly.

"I'm trying to see why you've haven't been answering my calls or texts."

"Who is this, Monsta?" the chick asked.

"None of your concern, sweetie. Now like I said why haven't you been answering my calls?"

"I didn't know I had to. Since you're here, have a seat and relax. All this negative energy you bringing to my section is killing my vibe. Here, have a drink."

"Nigga, fuck you and that drink."

He extended his hand and tried to hand me a champagne filled flute. I knocked that shit out his hand and made it go all over the bitch. Did he really think he was dealing with one of these bird brain ass bitches that be falling up behind him like a puppy? Then again that's exactly what it looked like. I walked away as fast as I could and out of that damn club.

"Serenity! Bring your ass here." I heard Jah calling me, but I kept walking towards my car. I was not in the mood for his bullshit. This nigga had me so fucked up. Moniece was right he was rude and arrogant as fuck.

"Bye, Jah." He must have put some pep up in his step because before I knew it. He was yanking me back. He roughly pushed up against my car and pressed his body against mine.

"Let's get some shit real clear. You're not fucking with one of these bitch ass niggas out here in these streets. I'm a motherfucking gangsta. Don't you ever disrespect me by knocking some shit out of my hand. The only reason I didn't fuck you up in there is because I fucks with you the long way. Now let's get some straight. You're not my bitch and we ain't official. When I'm with you, I'm with you, and when I'm not, I'm not. All this territorial shit is for the birds. Make this the last time you question me about anything I do. As a woman, you need to know your place. Now go home and wait for me, I'll be there when I can."

"I'm good, Jah. Stay away from me. I don't know why you came into my life and started fucking with me anyway. I'm grown as fuck, and you play too many mind games. You come into my life out of the blue and then just stop answering my calls. I'm lost as to what I did to you to make you just turn all cold towards me."

"I'm busy, Serenity. I can't just answer every time you call. I'm a busy ass man, and I have to be focused. Look, don't get me wrong I fucks with you, but we live two totally different lives. I'm a street nigga, and you're a good girl. I can assure you I'm not what you want. I'm a dog Serenity, and you don't deserve that. I love to have my pick of women. You see it's nothing you did, but sometimes I have to distance myself. If I'm around too much, then I'll have you thinking we're a couple or some shit. I just want to be honest. I'd rather tell you what it is from the jump instead of leading you on." He kissed me on the lips and walked away. I was confused as ever it was like he was a totally different person than he was three weeks ago.

"Get in the motherfucking car!" I turned around, and it was my father sitting in the backseat of his Maybach.

"Hey, Daddy! What's wrong with you?"

"What the fuck are you doing with that nigga Monsta?"

As we speeded out of the parking lot and passed the club, I locked eyes with Jah and his crew. He had a mean mug out of this world on his face. I had a feeling some shit was about to pop off, and I was in the middle of it.

"He's a friend. What's the problem?"

"The problem is that I'm beefing with that nigga. I have a private detective following him. Imagine my surprise when he showed me pictures of you fucking with this nigga, not to mention him coming out of your fucking house. Don't be no fool Serenity that nigga is using you to get to me."

"No, he's not Daddy. You aren't even a topic of discussion."

"That's because he's waiting for your ass to volunteer information. Stay the fuck away from him! Do you understand me?"

I think this man had forgotten that I was grown. I wanted to curse and tell him that but now wasn't the time. I was more concerned about if Jah was really using me to get to my father.

"Okay, Daddy."

"I'm going to drop you off at my home, but I'll be here bright and early to pick you up. Your ass is coming back to the estate so that I can keep an eye on you."

I wasn't in the mood to argue with him, so I just let him say whatever. About thirty minutes later he dropped me off at home. My head was killing me. I'm pretty sure it was the Remy plus Jah and my father's bullshit that had it hurting.

As I walked inside my home, I removed my shoes and flicked on the lights. Before I could say anything, Jah yanked me by the throat and slammed me into the wall. "I'm gone ask you one time and one time only. Are you spying on me for that nigga Money?"

The feeling of the cold steel pressed against my temple made me shed tears. I was so damn scared I was literally shaking.

"Noooo! What are you talking about?

"I'm talking about you being in the car with that nigga Money, the same bitch ass nigga that tried to have me killed. Are you fucking that nigga!" he said through gritted teeth.

"Noooo! That's my father!"

"You're fucking with me, right? Because you had better not be lying to me."

"I swear to God Jah. Money is my father, but I don't know about what he does in the streets. He keeps that part of his life away from me. I have no idea about what's going on between you two."

"Stay the fuck away from me and lose my fucking number!"

"Please Jah! You got it all wrong. I swear I wasn't trying to set you up. Just listen to me." I pleaded with him but I could tell he wasn't trying to hear it.

He removed the gun from my head and roughly pushed me away from him. I wanted to say something, but I was speechless. I slouched down to the floor and sat in silence trying figuring out what to do next.

MONSTA

When I got back into Dex's Beemer, I was so fucked up in the head. I laid my head back on the headrest because this revelation had a nigga fucked up.

"What's good, bro?"

"You know my nurse shawty that just spazzed out on me in the club? That's the nigga Money's daughter. How in the fuck did I not know that shit?" I started hitting the damn dashboard over and over. That shit had me livid. I had snoozed, which is something I never do. He got quiet for a minute before saying anything.

"What the fuck are you going to do?"

"I went to her fucking crib and threatening her ass. I told her to stay the fuck away from me. She was crying and trying to explain, but I wasn't trying to hear none of that shit." Dex was laughing and looking at me like I was crazy.

"Nigga, you're all in your feelings when you should be taking advantage of this shit. You need to continue fucking with her so that you can get leverage over her pops. She'll lead you right to his ass. All you need to do is be patient and fuck with her. From the way she acted tonight, I can tell she's feeling you. Listen to me my nigga, don't let this golden ticket slip through your hands."

I sat back in deep thought about what I wanted to do. He made perfect sense, and I didn't want to rush and go back into the house and switch from what I just told her. Instead, I decided to give it a few days before I speak with her again. Right now I had the upper hand, and I would use this time wisely. I needed to watch the nigga Money closer. Now that he knows I had been fucking with his daughter, he's definitely about to be in his feelings behind the shit. He really wants to murk my ass now. The feelings are definitely mutual. I remembered back when I vowed to get back at Money. This was way before I found out he had something to do with hitting me up

As Dex pulled the seven series Beemer back onto the road, I stared out of the window. The abandoned buildings and spray painted garage doors passed by quickly as he picked up speed. I closed my eyes and subconsciously went down memory lane.

I stood in pure disbelief and fear. I was on my way home from school when I heard my mother's voice. She was screaming at the top of her lungs telling someone to get off of her. When I heard my mother's mouth, I immediately made my feet work faster. As I got closer to where she was outside, I saw her pushing a tall black dude wearing three really big gold chains. I damn near jumped out of my skin when I saw him kick the shit out of her boyfriend at the time, Elroy Jackson. I couldn't help but notice a loud Puerto Rican chick who was standing next to a midnight black Acura Legend. She and mother looked like they were in a heated argument. All I remembered was my mother taking two steps, and then the next thing you know moms was on top of the bitch giving her the business.

Then out of nowhere, I heard a loud boom that erupted through the air. The man with all of the chains had shot Elroy in the head. Everything moved in slow motion as I watched my mother lunge at him. Before she could get close to him, he let off two shots in my mother's head. He picked up the Puerto Rican girl that was fighting my mother and placed her inside of the car. He hopped in the driver's seat and sped away. The nigga killed my mother and Elroy. He left them in the middle of the street like trash. I was in a daze looking at the blood pool around my mother's head. A woman noticed me and started calling my name. That's when everyone in the streets realized I had seen my mother murdered. I don't know why I just took off

42

running with people calling my name. I never looked back I just kept running.

"Yo! Nigga! You sleep, fam?"

"Nah, nah… I'm straight. Take me to the crib."

It was amazing how that shit still played in my head daily. It was like the shit had just happened. During my mother's funeral, I heard whispers about who had done it. It was then I found out it was a nigga named Money. It wasn't hard for me to find out who he was. He ran the streets of the A. Nothing could move unless he said it could move. I was young as hell, but from the moment I saw that motherfucker kill my mother, I vowed to get him back.

I hate thinking about the day that snake motherfucker took my mother away from me. It's his fault why I ended up having such a fucked up childhood. I was sent to live with my grandmother, and that shit was hell. I spent my days trying to protect myself from her gay, pedophile ass husband. It seemed as though he loved little boys. I couldn't talk to anybody about it, and my mother didn't raise no pussy. I refused to live in fear of this nigga molesting me. I had been coming up with all types of shit to steer clear of this sick mother-fucker. I knew it wouldn't be long before he managed to fuck with me. My grandmother played blind to a lot of shit, so I decided to open up her eyes.

I didn't even give a fuck it hurt her very existence. I refused to let that nigga fuck with me, so I poisoned the nigga with rat poison. Over the course of a week, I slowly put that shit in all of his Cognac. He loved to drink so I knew that's how I could get him. He had been waking up sick every day up until he just didn't wake up. I couldn't believe I had caught my first body at thirteen. It was then I realized that I had the power to make people go away for fucking with me.

I believe that my grandmother was aware I was responsible for her husband's death. Years after his death, she would always say that he told her that I would be trouble. She hated coming up to the school for me. It was like after my mother died, I didn't give a fuck about anything.

Eventually, she said she was tired of having to leave her job. She was losing out on money constantly coming up to the school for me. Since she had no one to help her with me, she decided to give me to the state. It was fucked up that she told me it would be better for me. Talking about I would thank her later in life. I wish she was alive to tell her lazy ass that she was dead wrong. It actually fucked me up even more. I remembered running away every time I could until they made the school monitors keep a special eye on me. Once I was in high school, I only went to school to fuck with the bitches and throw dice. I never gave a fuck about learning anything. All I ever wanted was to grow up and be vicious enough to kill the motherfucker that killed my mother.

There were a few times I came close to his camp. I was never successful at getting close to him though. I have to give it to him. He keeps his security on lock, and the nigga is hard to kill. I never knew or have ever heard that this nigga had a daughter. I look at his black ass complexion compared to Serenity's complexion, and she definitely has to look like her mother. I realize that she bears a strong resemblance to the Spanish chick I saw my mother fighting that day the more I think about it. Even after all of these years, I can still see her face vividly.

Damn, how did I miss the fact that this nigga had a daughter? A slight feeling of intimidation came over me, but I quickly brushed it away. The feeling of intimidation came about because he knew about me fucking with his daughter, and I didn't know she was his daughter.

"Bruh, since we pulled off, this burgundy Toyota two cars behind have been following us," Dex said, looking in the rearview mirror.

"Get on the highway and merge onto I-20 west. It's dark when you first get on the bridge. As you get on, pull over on the shoulder, and turn all the lights off. If he gets on this highway that's a tail and I want you to pull up beside it." I was giving him directions but keeping an eye on the car behind us as well.

Just like I thought it was a tail. When the car passed us, it was too late. We made eye contact with the two niggas. Dex pulled up beside them, and I let off all twenty-two rounds from the FN into the Toyota. They lost control, ran off of the highway, and hit a tree head on. It was no question that both men were dead. I broke the gun down and threw pieces of the gun out the window every quarter mile until the gun was gone.

We pulled off on Flat Shoals and pulled into the car wash. We cleaned the car making sure to get all of the shells that had dropped in the car. When we were finished a half hour later, we decided to go to the Sky Bar to get a drink or two. We also did so that we could have our faces on somebody's camera system. Despite all of the night's events and the way shit had turned out, I couldn't help but think of Serenity. No woman ever had this type of effect on me.

* * *

A FEW DAYS later I decided to call Serenity, but she had changed her number. I called her job, and she was on leave. I went by her house, but she wasn't there. I doubled back around the time I knew she would be home, but she still wasn't there. Then it dawned on me that Money now knows that I know that's his daughter. He is going to make it difficult for me to get in contact with her. This was all bad, and I'm sure his bitch ass was already trying to turn her against me.

Just when I was about to make my way up to the hospital to see if I can get some answers, my phone rang. It was my lil' partner Mark telling me that G-baby's momma's funeral was today. I rushed to my garage like a bat out of hell. I got my .50 caliber sniper rifle and loaded it up inside of the car. I drove like a bat out of hell trying to make it to the funeral.

By the time I made it to the funeral, they were placing the casket inside of the hearse. I knew then I would have to catch his bitch ass at the cemetery. The gravesite was about a mile away from the funeral home. I decided to take a different route to get inside of the cemetery so that I could set up my scope. I could see the cars turning into the cemetery from the other side. I anxiously waited to see that nigga emerge from one of the family cars. About two minutes later, I was happy as fuck when I saw people emerging from the vehicles. I zoomed in, and it was my man, G 'motherfucking' baby!

I waited until he went to assist the other pallbearers with pulling the casket out of the hearse. As they took their first couple of steps, I squeezed the stiff trigger. The gun spit the huge bullet out of its long nozzle with an extreme blast. When it connected with the pallbearer next to G-baby, it took his head off, but before the casket drop I squeezed the trigger again and knocked G-baby off both legs then bore a hole through his heart. Satisfied with the mayhem I just carried out, I pulled away like I had done nothing. All of the commotion going on with the mourners helped me to get away without anyone noticing where the shots came from. I was pleased and feeling accomplished that I murdered the motherfucker who tried to murder me.

SERENITY

*J*t had been a month since I had heard from Jah. After our last encounter, he had spoken to me so bad that I was afraid to be around him. He had this look in his eyes that let me know he would have pulled the trigger if he even had an inkling that I was lying. His crazy ass had me so shook that I took a leave of absence from work. To add insult to injury my father and his goons showed up at my house the morning after the incident. He basically snatched my ass up and made me move back home. As much as I wanted to fight with him, I know it wasn't a good idea.

Since this shit with Jah has come to light, he has been on a war path. I've been hiding out in the guest house because I get tired of him breaking shit and cursing, not to mention taking his frustrations out on Kee Baby. I never knew that he put his hands on her. She's been hiding this shit well. Something is terribly wrong with my father. Never in all of my years have I seen him act out in any way. That only makes me want to find out why he and Jah are beefing so hard. There has to be some logical explanation as to why they're out for blood.

* * *

"DID you know that motherfucker killed Nas?" I jumped up in bed from the sound of my father's booming voice. I had to gather myself because he had just woke me up out of my sleep.

"No! I didn't know that, " I lied quickly as hell. Of course, I wasn't going to tell him that I knew Jah was responsible for Nas murder.

"It's a lot of shit you don't know about him. Listen to me and listen to me good. Stay the fuck away from that nigga and anybody that's affiliated with him. If you even think about fucking with that fuck nigga you're dead to me."

He quickly walked out of the bedroom and out of the guest house. I shook my head in disbelief and jumped up to put on my clothes. I was done with this shit. I'm twenty-five years old I shouldn't even be explaining anything. I'm grown as fuck and being kept in a guest house like a child. This isn't even about Jah at this point for me. This is about him not respecting me as an adult.

After I got dressed, I walked into my father's house through the kitchen door. He and Kee were sitting at the table eating breakfast.

"Look, I respect you as my father, but I need for you to respect me. You don't get to keep me locked up like some damn princess in the tower. I'm grown Daddy, and I have my own everything. Now I understand you and Jah—"

"Let me cut you off right there. Make that the last time you speak that fuck niggas name out of your mouth. It's funny that you say his government name instead of his street name Monsta. You in love with that nigga, huh? Baby girl, I hate to break it to you, but he doesn't love you. He was just using you to get to me. I advise you to get over whatever feelings you have for him because he won't be on this Earth much longer."

"Really, Money? Don't you think you can be a little bit more sensitive to her feelings? She's in the middle of something she has no idea about. That's not fair to her. She's still your daughter no matter whom she's involved with."

"Shut the fuck up!" Before I could catch him, he had reached across the table and slapped the shit out of her. I just knew she was going to jump up and hit his ass back. Instead, she just held her face and walked out.

"Daddy, why would you hit her like that. I can't believe you. I'm so disappointed in you right now. If I make you mad will you start putting your hands on me too?"

"Don't question me about shit. You came out my nut sack. Like the fuck I said, stay away from that nigga Monsta, or you won't like the outcome." He flipped the table over and walked out of the kitchen. I was happy as hell when he went out of the door because I wanted to go and check on Keelah.

When I walked into their bedroom, she was sitting at the vanity putting on makeup. I just knew I was going to come in there and find her crying her eyes out. I'm honestly surprised her damn head is still attached to her body because he slapped the fuck out of her. Like the shit sounded off so loud that I felt the shit in my soul.

"Are you okay?"

"Oh yeah! I'm fine. He's just upset with all of this stuff that's going on. Your daddy has a temper. He'll be okay once he calms down. He'll be so sorry that he'll buy me whatever I want or send me to trip out of the country. Knowing your daddy, he's at the jewelry store or the dealership as we speak."

Shocked was an understatement listening to her. I just couldn't believe that she thought his gifts made it okay for putting his hands on her. This incident added with him threatening me was enough for me to get the hell out of there.

"I'm sorry for him putting his hands on you. That shit wasn't right."

That was about all I could say. There was no need for me to be concerned about her if she didn't care about herself. I walked over and hugged her tight before I walked out of the room. I didn't even take anything. I left my father's house with what the hell I had on my back.

About an hour later, I was pulling up to my house. Before I could even get inside of my house, two big ass niggas in all black snatched me up. I couldn't see their faces because they were rocking ski masks. I started to panic when they placed a black bag over my head.

"Ahhhhhhhh! Let me go!" I started screaming and fighting like hell to get out of their grasp, but they held on to me tight. I felt myself being lifted up and carried. I knew that they were stuffing my ass in the trunk of a car because they had to adjust my body so it could fit.

"Stop all that damn screaming. All of this shit will be over soon."

"Please let me go!" My begging and pleading were useless. I heard the trunk slam, and I immediately began to panic. The smell of gasoline and the low quality of air started to make me claustrophobic.

I was trying my best to calm down because the more I moved around in the trunk, the more tired I became. As the car drove, it seemed as if they were going over every damn pot hole or rough ass street. That had to be on a damn back road. The busier streets weren't this damn raggedy. The car wasn't even driving that long before it came to a complete stop. My heart began to race hearing the slamming of the car doors. Tears seeped from my eyes. As I heard the footsteps coming nearer, I started to cry. The trunk opened, and I was lifted out of it. The feeling of me being thrown over someone's shoulders made me start kicking and screaming. If I was about to die, I for damn sure wasn't going out like no weak bitch.

"Stop all that damn fighting. Your ass hits hard, girl. Now I'm going to take this damn thing off your head. Start screaming and I'm going to make my mans shoot you." He didn't have to tell me twice I shut the fuck up because I was trying to get out of this alive. He removed the bag off of my head, and one of the guys in the ski mask stood in front of me.

"So, this what I have to do to find you," Jah said as he removed his ski mask.

MONSTA

I could tell by the look in her eyes that she was beyond amazed that it was me behind of her abduction. I had fucked her head up even more with this move here. That was my intention from the jump. Serenity needed to know what and who the fuck she was dealing with.

"What the hell Jah?"

"This is my city lil' mama. You entered my world, and it's not big enough for you to hide from me. I'm gone ask you right now who side are you on? This is the only time I would show you mercy because I know you ain't ask for this. I also know how delicate the situation is, so either way, I'll be proud of you. However, if you say yes to me and then deceive me I won't spare you my wrath, do you understand me?"

I watched as she shook her head in agreement.

"Are you sure because there is no turning back at this point?"

"Yes. I'm sure. The fact that she was picking lust and love over family said a lot about her character. It made me wonder about her relationship with her father and what she has endured through her life that would make her choose me.

I had my Bentley truck parked on the other side of the garage. I walked her to my truck and opened the door for her. I jumped into the truck and drove us to Hartsfield-Jackson International. She looked puzzled as to why we were at the airport parking. I opened the back door and grabbed my Fendi book bag.

I held her hand and guided her to the Delta Airlines section. I ordered two first class business trip tickets to Tokyo. It was a place I always dreamed of going before I died, and with all the shit that was going on this is the best time for a getaway to create memories.

"Baby, I'm not sure about this. I don't even have my passport."

"Relax, I got you covered."

She looked so nervous and out of place. I knew I had to pull out all the stops to secure her decision. We made it past customs without any issues, and forty-five minutes later, we were lifting off into the air on our way to Tokyo.

* * *

FIFTEEN HOURS LATER, we landed in Japan. I had preordered a Rolls Royce Ghost to pick us up when we landed. After I had seen the driver with the black hat and suit holding my name, I walked up to him and took the keys out of his hand. We jumped into the Ghost, and before I pulled off, I had to reprogram it to English because the worst feeling in the world is to be lost in a different country that doesn't speak the same language as you do.

A half hour later, we were pulling up into this prestigious like city. It was like New York's Times Square times ten. The city was filled with lights; the streets looked brand new and jet black. The buildings were designed differently— it seemed like only one culture existed here.

Eventually, the GPS brought us in front of the valet at the Hilton Tokyo Odaiba. The presidential suite that I reserved cost me ten thousand American dollars. We were both in awe when we were taken into the room; it was so huge. As weird as it is for me to say this, it was beautiful. It was unlike anything I've ever seen. She was breathless, to say the least. I sat back and watched as she walked all around the suite taking in everything.

I knew we needed clothes and shit, so I told her to go ahead and get in the shower and put on the same shit on we came with. I was glad that the hotel came with translators. The translator gave me all the information I needed about the sights of the city. Since I wasn't sure about shopping out there, I had a designer and tailor come to the room. Because Serenity didn't have any clothes, I had to make sure she matched my fly. While Serenity was being fitted, I decided to go out and grab us a couple of things for the room.

By the time I made it back upstairs, bae was in the bathroom butt naked looking like fresh bread. I leaned up against the doorway as she oiled her skin. She sang loudly to "Do Me Baby" by the great Prince. She was feeling the music so much that she didn't even realize I was standing there admiring her womanly curves. Her beauty was an event, and it was almost intoxicating.

When she noticed me, I saw the tiger in her eyes when we made eye contact. She smirked mischievously.

"How long were you standing there?'

"Not long enough."

I looked on as she slowly walked passed me never breaking eye contact. It was obvious that with every step she takes her firm body jiggled in all the right places automatically hypnotizing me. I looked as she passed me and her perfect ass cheeks wobbled together. I knew if I put my hands on her like she is begging me too, we wouldn't make it out the room. We'll get around to fucking each other's brains out. My goal right now is to blowing her mind and making her feel secure. She chose her love for me over her father's, so I felt like I needed to do whatever to reassure her that she's made the right choice. I know it's a lot on her. I can tell each and every time I catch her staring off at the wall in deep thought. I needed to make her comfortable and show my appreciation.

A knock at the door interrupted my lustful thoughts. I walked to the door forgetting that I had called the tailor upstairs for me. The American woman walked in with racks of suits and other clothes for me. After going through the clothes, I chose a gray pin striped double breasted suit by Tom Ford. She pulled out some matching Tom Ford loafers that set the suit off. The finishing touch was the diamond cuff-links she added. I was in the game and ready. A nigga was looking and feeling like a million bucks. After choosing some more pieces, the tailor left. When I returned to the room to get dressed, Serenity was dressed and looking beautiful as fuck.

She was rocking a peach colored dress from Roberto Cavalli. She was looking like a real life Barbie. I wanted to tear it off of her, but she was too beautiful for all of that. I was so happy she didn't have all that makeup on. I loved a woman who had natural beauty, not bitches who be looking casket sharp in the face.

We decided on the restaurant Aronia de Takazawa. It was one of the fancier restaurants with an intimate setting. It literally only set about eight people a night. Serenity and I took a spot towards the back so that we can have privacy.

"This is so nice. I've never been anywhere like this." Serenity was looking around the room in awe.

"Me either. This shit dope as fuck."

"Thank you so much for getting me away from it all, even though you committed a damn felony to do it." She laughed and sipped from her wine glass.

"Hey, a nigga's got to do what a nigga's got to do." I winked at her and made her blush.

It was then I noticed that she only had one dimple. Serenity was beautiful as fuck. It was the little things that really made me notice her beauty and her inner soul. There is no way she could be Money's daughter. I was just having a hard time believing it.

After drinking two bottles of wine, we left the restaurant to take in the sights. Everything looked so futuristic. We stopped in front of this building that a huge fish tank with all types of exotic fishes in it. The way her eyes lit up made a nigga feel good as fuck.

She wanted to walk through the city and enjoy the night. We were taking hella pictures, and I made her promise not to post them until we made it back to the United States.

This was the first time I was somewhere and didn't need a gun or felt like I had to look over my shoulder. It felt good to be alive and live care free. It dawned on me at that time that I had nothing to prove and had enough money to move to like London or Jamaica or something where nobody knows us and start over. But, that thought was quickly pushed to the back of my mind after the thought of reading Robert Greens *The 48 Laws Of Power*, which boldly states that one should crush the enemy to no return. To let him live maybe a vital mistake. I quickly pushed that thought out of my mind and proceeded back to the car.

When I got to the car, I realized for the first time in a long time I felt happy. It was weird because I know it wasn't Tokyo, but more so who I was in Tokyo with. For one moment I wasn't Monsta, I was Jah. Reality quickly set in when my business phone started going off with messages from my crew. My spots had been hit. So, much for enjoying my damn vacation.

SERENITY

apan had been everything the short time we were there. I had never been out of the country, so it felt good being around another culture. Not to mention being in a different setting around Jah. He was a totally different person. The way he was acting and treating me was all brand new. It didn't seem like a month ago he was threatening my life at gunpoint. I didn't understand what the fuck I was doing. My mind was telling me to get far away from Jah while my heart was telling me to choose him like he wanted. At the same time, I felt like I was betraying my father by choosing him. It wasn't like that at all, though. I was choosing Jah because that's what I wanted. I loved my father, but I wasn't going to let him choose who I can be with.

The whole ride home on the plane I thought about what my father must be thinking of me. I let a few tears fall, but I quickly wiped them away. I didn't want Jah to see me crying.

I was exhausted after the long plane ride. I kept trying to engage in conversation with Jah, but he was blowing me off. Instead of getting mad or feeling some type of way, I decided to give him his space. I knew that he was angry about whatever had kicked off back home while we were in Japan. He made sure not to speak on the phone in front of me, and that made me feel like he was up to something. Either that or my father was behind whatever was going on. I decided to just go with the flow of things and not worry about his street business.

"This is nice," I said as I walked around his luxurious Buckhead condo. It was obvious he was obsessed with elephants and the Buddha. It was all white everything and looked like he barely lived in it.

"I'm glad you like it. Come here let me show you something."

He grabbed me by the hand and led me to the back of the house to the master bedroom. My eyes got big looking at all of my things placed strategically throughout the room. Not to mention the walk in closet that held brand new clothes he had got for me along with all of my old things

"How did all of my things get here?"

"Don't worry about the small shit. Just get comfortable this is your home now."

"Wait a minute; I don't think that's a good idea."

"That's why you need to let me do the thinking. Don't worry. Let me handle everything. Look I got some shit I need to handle. Get comfortable. I'll be back when I can." Jah kissed me on the forehead and walked out of the door.

I knew that I should have spoken up about him just moving my stuff out of my house. This is all moving too fast. My mind started to overthink and wonder about if Jah was being genuine, or if he had an ulterior motive. *Maybe he's using me to get back at my father.* I thought to myself.

My heart raced as I headed towards the front door.

"Where are you going?"

"Who are you?" I asked the big fat ass nigga that was sitting on the couch eating a big ass burger. I rolled my eyes looking at the mustard in the crack of his mouth.

"I'm Biggs. I'm on security just in case you tried to do what you're doing now. Take your ass back there and don't try to leave. Jah made it perfectly clear that you are not to leave this house. Are you trying to get me and you fucked up?"

"I wasn't going to leave. I was trying to catch Jah, but it's obvious I'm too late." I rolled my eyes and walked back to the bedroom.

I made sure to lock the door behind me. He looked like a fat ass creep. I wasn't taking no chances with his ass. I became mad at Jah for leaving his fat ass here with me. Since I was going to be here for awhile, I decided to get comfortable. I went inside of the dresser drawer and found a pretty white lace camisole and panty set. I was surprised it was the right size. After soaking in the huge Jacuzzi tub, I oiled my body with coconut oil and climbed up in the bed. The California King bed was so huge that it basically swallowed my ass. As I found my comfortable spot, I felt like I could get used to this life. I opened my eyes and looked over at the empty side of the bed and wondering when Jah was coming back.

* * *

I WOKE up in the middle of the night and looked over at Jah knocked out in all black. For a minute, I stared at him as he slept. I wondered what type of hell he had raised in the streets. I know he had done something because those weren't the clothes he left in. I raised up and went inside of the bathroom to rinse my mouth. As I walked back towards the bed, I couldn't help but laugh at Jah snoring. I sat on the floor in front of him, and I removed the Timbs he had on his feet. I removed his socks, and then I pulled off his Nike joggers. I couldn't believe he didn't budge while I removed his clothes. His silk Versace boxers looked sexy as hell on him. The bulge in his shorts had me horny as fuck. I don't know what it is about his dick, but it was made perfectly. I swear the head was shaped like a huge mushroom. My mouth watered at the very thought of it. I don't know what came over me, but I got up on my knees and slipped my hand inside of his boxers. Even in its soft state, it was thick. I managed to pull out his dick, and I placed the head in my mouth and sensually sucked on the head. The feeling of him stirring around made me go down further. It slowly swelled up in my mouth as he began to fuck my face. I was on some slow sensual shit, but he was on some rough fuck my face type of shit. My eyes watered and I gagged as he held the back of my head tight and fucked my mouth. He was doing the shit so rough that I knew my damn throat was going to be sore afterwards.

"Fuckkkk!" he groaned. I felt the veins swell up in my mouth and I just knew he was about to burst. Instead, he roughly grabbed me by the hair and lifted me up.

"What's wrong?"

"Bend your ass over!" he commanded. I did like I was told. Before I could get bent over good enough, he was ripping my pants off and pushing my face into the bed.

"Ahhhhhh!" I screamed out as he roughly pounded in and out of me.

I thought I would go crazy when he slipped a finger into my ass. I was losing my mind as he fucked the shit out of me. I felt like I was pissing on myself. That's how wet he had me. I was out of breath and trying my best to grab onto anything I could just to keep my balance. The way he was fucking me, I felt like I was going to collapse at any minute. This nigga was an animal. No, let me rephrase that, he was a monster, and he was giving me that Monsta dick. I swear this nigga was snatching my soul with each thrust. It had been a minute since I had some dick, but I wasn't about to let him think I was a lazy fuck.

I started to bounce that ass all on his dick. As soon as I got into it, he gripped my waist and basically held me in position so that I couldn't move. After he had come inside of me long and hard, he smacked me on the ass and pulled out of me. I didn't have the strength to do anything after that I climbed in the bed on the side where I was and fell asleep.

MONSTA

*J*t's been three days that I've been trying to get in contact with Dex. I had a plan but needed him to help me execute it. The way things are set up right now in the streets with Money and me I don't trust anyone with what I got planned except for Dex. I'm starting to worry bout bro because this would be the first time ever he haven't returned my call. I had a bad vibe in the pit of my stomach, but I didn't want to give into any negative form of thinking especially with this war I'm in the middle of. Serenity was starting to piss me the fuck off. Every minute she was trying to find a way to get out of the house, which I'm starting to believe she is willingly neglecting the fact that she recently betrayed the man that killed my mother in front of me. I have to keep reminding myself that she doesn't know about that, though. I practically have the only thing that is pure to him, and the only thing he could have trust and love truly in my possession.

In the streets that made him look fucked up, and I know he would stop at nothing to take her back any way he can and in the process, she may lose her life. She was as hard headed as any other woman, but I was at least expecting her to understand the depth of this situation that we are in. She needed not to underestimate her father's ability to

60

kill. When a man feels as if his ego or pride has been attacked, he wouldn't rest at anything to restore his image.

Money is a ruthless nigga, he the type of nigga that would put a hit on a kid to prove a point. Back in the day, I heard he had a basement they called The Area Fifty One, and to this day no one knows if this place truly exists. It was rumored that Money and his crew would take niggas that owed money or those who were simply on the wrong side of the tracks. He would torture them, and even sometimes covering their bodies with peanut butter so that the rats would eat them alive. I was a beast out here in these streets with my murder game, but Money was no joke about his shit either.

This is why I needed Dex to answer his phone and get back at me like yesterday. My plan was to go at this nigga Money with everything I had even using Serenity as a pawn. I know she would be mad and probably wouldn't understand, but I'll go through hell and high water to make it up to her though. Bottom line he had to go and this nigga Dex was holding up this nigga eviction notice off this earth.

I looked at babe lying in bed with just my tank top on. Right there and then I knew God had blessed me with my very own personal angel. The only question I'll have for God is how the fuck a nigga like Money produced a woman so pure and virtuous. She definitely didn't deserve him as a father or me as her nigga. We both had the potential to turn something so pure into something evil. Street niggas are notorious for fucking up a good girl's life.

I decided to go and find my partner. It's only three places he could have been— at his spot in Buckhead, his shop, or at his other spot in Fulton county. I decided to check his condo in Buckhead. He's been spending more time there ever since he hooked up with this bitch he met at Follies. I also had a key to get into the condo. It was pretty much where we brought the sliders to smash. I decided to drive my brand new cocaine white Corvette Stingray. I had never driven it since I bought it like four months ago, it was a beautiful day, and I needed to relax and think a bit. I screwed the top off the vet and made my way up I-285 north. On my way to Buckhead, it's like my stomach was in knots with the worst thoughts of why the fuck bro haven't even text me back. I called all the local jails and hospitals, but nothing came up. When I got to the condo, I opened the door, and everything was in order. While I was in Tokyo with Serenity, I had spoken to him once or twice. When we did speak, I explained to him I was turning my phone off, so he was in charge of everything only because I wanted to give babe the undivided attention that she deserved. The last thing I got from bro was a text the day before we were set to be back in the United States. The text was simple,

"Bruh, I hope yall enjoying y'all selves. I'm bout to head out to club Blaze get at me when you touch down."

I couldn't even deny the fact that I was a bit shaken up by his absence. This shit was weighing on me heavy and the fact that the condo was spotless, only made my heart beat even harder than it was already.

I got back into my Vet, and I could no longer ignore how fucked up this shit was. I'm a very impatient man as it is and it was obvious to the on lookers by the way I pulled out the parking lot that I was in a hurry. As I sped up I-20 west to get to the garage, I couldn't help but feel like the worst has happened, and if I did find bro, it wasn't going to be good. I quickly pushed that thought out of my mind and tried my best to think positive. Maybe bro was laid up with some new lil' bitch that had him feeling like he was in love again. Bro was a sucker for a pretty face, caramel complexion, and a big butt.

I hate that I was thinking the worst like I didn't know bro was a cold trick for a pretty bitch and with his ass he liable to be on a cruise somewhere with some new bitch he met yesterday. I smile at the thought of that fact being very factual, and it might be the case while I'm worried. I really needed to dead this whole Money shit because that shit's got me thinking the worst about everything.

I arrived at the garage forty minutes later and on yet another blank mission because he wasn't there. I was walking out of the garage feeling disappointed when I saw some red rims poking out from under the car cover. I didn't realize it, but on the way out, it just stuck out to me. I thought bro had left it in Pensacola. I walked over to the car, remove the cover, and saw that it was the cranberry red Donk

Seven Tray Impala he was working on for the past two years. It was hard as fuck looking at it. The paint job was wet as fuck, and right then and there I wish he was standing beside me to give me the technical update on the upgrade he had put into the car. This is what he lived for— to turn nothing into something.

I walked around the back of the Donk to see what he did with the tail pipes and shit, and I noticed spots of blood on the floor and on the bumper. It was like four or five spots, and I've seen enough blood to know that it truly was blood. At that time, it was like hearing my heart thudding inside of my chest cavity, I walked around to the driver side to checked the door, and it was open. I reached for the lever for the trunk and pulled it. I heard the trunk opened and I took deep slow breaths as I made my way around to the trunk of the Impala.

When I opened the trunk all the way, it confirmed my worst fears. I stood looking over the body of my childhood friend. It was obvious that he was tortured. His finger nails were plucked off. He was naked and decapitated with his head in his lap, and his dick in his own mouth. His body was already decomposing due to the heat and shit it was stink as a motherfucker, but that never made me move an inch. I was in shock. It was like I was reliving the same pain I felt when my moms died. The only difference was bro and his family was the ones there for me, and now he is gone because of me. I looked on as tears flowed freely down my face as I stood there and took in everything. That motherfucker did this to my best friend and the nigga I call my brother.

His head was swollen in his lap. His skin was turning gray, and his blood was now almost black and tar like. His hands were now swollen to the point boils were visible around the wrist where they were tied. I could tell that he suffered long before he died. They probably killed him after they realize he was gone die how he lived— solid as a rock.

I eventually made the call to 911 and disappeared from the scene. I went back to my house got a couple hundred thousand together and had it sent off to his mother, Paulette. I didn't want to be the one to tell her, and I know she will deeply hate me for what happened to her only baby boy. I wouldn't blame her though because I blamed me also.

After I had sent the money out, I stared at Serenity as she slept without a care in the world. With my Springfield 1911 edition .45 grip tight in my hand beside me, I looked on at her with hate. For the first time just wanting to hurt something close to that nigga, just wanting him for once to feel my fucking pain and all that he has robbed me of.

I pointed the gun at her head, and for the first time, my hand trembled in this position. For the first time I felt lost, and for the first time, I didn't know what I was doing. I rapidly turned the gun on myself feeling hopeless and defeated. I then broke down. I let it the fuck out because it was killing me. All the pain and hurt I was harboring within me was only deteriorating my heart and sanity. I screamed from the depths of my soul startling Serenity out of her sleep. She jumped up and rushed to my side as I cried like a newborn. She never asked me what was wrong; she only encouraged me to let it out and not to fight it. She felt warm, and her words were soothing. It was hard to explain to her that this pain that I was feeling, and that I had always felt, was due to the man that brought her into this world. Because of this motherfucker, I've suffered greatly.

The last thing I could remember was feeling Serenity warm tears drip onto my face as if she already knew who was responsible for all of the pain that I was currently experiencing. My body then went light, and my vision blanked out.

SERENITY

I swear I was running out of my patience being held up in Jah's house. Since Dex had been killed, he had been on the warpath. Unfortunately, I just happened to be one of the people that he was taking his anger out on. I didn't know if it was because of him mourning the loss of his friend or my father being the one who most likely killed him. Either way, he was taking his anger out on me, and I was tired of his shit.

He was drinking fifths of Remy daily and smoking weed by the pound. I hated when he was intoxicated because his senses heightened, and he was mean as fuck. I was happy it was time for me to head back to work. That way I wouldn't be around him twenty-four seven, and I could see Moniece. I felt so bad because he forbid me to talk to her. Let him tell it she's not to be trusted. Moniece is cool, and I know that she would never tell my business. I don't know if I should believe him, but he said that Moniece was mad because he wouldn't let her suck his dick in the hospital. That don't even sound like the way she rolls. I have every intention of asking he though. That shit don't sit well with me at all.

I really wanted to curse him the fuck out, but I decided to go another route. The more I was around him, the more I learned him.

He was very meticulous about everything— from the thread count of his sheets to the temperature the iron was on when his clothes were ironed. It was weird to me. I had never seen anything like it before. I found myself looking around his home and realizing there was no life in it. Most homes had pictures of family, but he had none at all. The only thing that was in existence were expensive paintings. I was so intrigued by his paintings from Picasso. Imagine that, a thug ass nigga with Picasso's on his wall.

I tried making small talk about his family, but he immediately shut the conversation down. It was then I realized that I knew nothing about Jah. I think that was the problem. I should have been trying to get to know Monsta. It was obvious that's who he was. Throughout the duration of the time I had been here, I've seen him get rid of so many bloody clothes. Some of his shoes have even had blood droplets on them. I simply got rid of them. The shit in the streets was getting out of hand because he was getting sloppy. He might think I'm green, but I'm far from it. Although I would love to be more hands on with him, I know that he will never let me.

I had been thinking of my father a lot lately and wondering what he must think of me. I know he's thinking I betrayed him, but I didn't. The more I thought about it, the more I wanted to reach out to him. I had to find a way to get out of the house so that I could go see him. I could never live with myself knowing that. At the same time, I didn't want Jah thinking I was having second thoughts about choosing him.

* * *

"CAN I COME TOO?" Jah was packing his bags for a last minute business trip.

"No. I'll be back Sunday. Just hold shit down here for a nigga until I touch back down."

I pouted because that was the last thing I wanted him to say. I absolutely hated being in his house when he was gone. I knew that he was going to leave me here with that fat fuck.

"Don't do that. I'll be back before you know it. Come hop in the shower so I can give you some dick. You'll be okay after that." I couldn't do anything but laugh because it most definitely was true. This nigga had a bitch dickmatized.

Hours later Jah was gone, and I was patiently waiting for Biggs to go his fat ass to sleep. I was lying in bed exchanging texts with Moniece. She was on her way to scoop me so that I could get out and get some air. What she didn't know was that I really didn't want to get some air. I wanted her to take me to see my father. I was scared and nervous at the same time. Jah was going to kill me when he finds out I left the house. I would have to deal with his wrath later. Right now this was about confronting my father instead of running away without handling the situation.

I looked at the clock, and I realized it was midnight. After throwing on a pair of jeans and a white t-shirt, I tip-toed into the living room to see if Biggs was sleep. I almost passed out looking at a masked gun man holding a gun to his head. Biggs looked like he was about to shit on himself. I tried to step closer, but I was pulled from the back, and my mouth was immediately covered. At the same time, I watched in horror as the gun man pulled the trigger and Biggs thoughts was splattered against the wall behind him.

"You've been a bad little girl," a deep husky male voice whispered in my ear.

I took notice of the strong scent of Big Red gum. My heart began to race because I knew the only person it could be was my father's henchman Domo. He only sends him when he wants him to do damage. I know that my father was mad at me for leaving. However, I didn't think that he would be so mad that he would have me killed.

MONSTA

Shit was getting wild in Atlanta and to be honest I was losing more men than anything else, and it was fucking with me more than I thought it would.

I know it was time for me to go see my dad. Well, the man that I considered to be my dad at least. Polo was the only father figure in my life after my mother's death. I guess they were dating at the time. From what I've heard, they grew up together, but Polo going back and forth to prison kept them apart, and he felt like it was his responsibility to look out for me. Nonetheless, a year later after my mother's death, he got picked up by the Feds for a chain of bank robberies he and his crew had hit throughout the city. Polo was a real nigga and is still well respected in the streets. To this day, his name is mentioned with much respect and among the greatest of street legends. When I walked into Big Sandy, a federal maximum facility, it kind of woke me up. *I know I needed to get my shit together and quickly because I'd hate to end up in this motherfucker*, is all I could think of myself.

Fortunately, because Polo was down so long, he had a lot of pull throughout the Bureau of Prisons. I still had to get searched and what not, but we were able to have contact visit in a private room, a secure room. When I saw Polo, my heart got heavy. He was aging on me. His dreads were now on the floor, and the top of his head fully gray along with his beard, but the fire in his eyes was still present. He still walked like he was the king of all kings. I smiled to myself but couldn't deny that he aged a lot since the last time I saw him.

"How are you holding up, big homie?"

"I'm holding. I'm worried about how you're holding up because you look like shit!" He said as he took his seat and encouraged me to take mines.

"Yea, I know fam! But I'm here because I'm going through it with that OG Money."

"I knew this day would come, and I can't say that I'm surprised, how did y'all cross paths?"

"Long story, but I'm fucking with his daughter. I didn't know she was his daughter but let's just say that shit took things to another level."

I looked around before I whispered that he even killed my main mans Dex. I studied Polo's face as he digested everything. With all I just told him, he seemed to be in deep thought. He wiped his hand over his face and placed his palms into a pyramid.

"Jah, you know I love you like a son, and because I do, I'm going be brutally honest with you. You stuck your hand in the mouth of a crocodile, and the only way to walk away with your hand and life is to move in silence and patience. You said that you're in love with his daughter and she is too, correct?"

"Well..."

"Ain't no well, you do love that girl son, and I can tell, but let me put this in your ear. Sometimes the things you love may have to get sacrificed in order for you to maintain, you dig? What I'm saying is, if you're not ready to die or to give her up completely, you only have three options. One is to run— but that's not in your blood line, the next is to use her as bait, and the other is to get rid of her so that you can focus on taking him out, after all, that is her father. Have you thought about the lengths that she may take to revenge his death? Son, once an enemy may never be a friend. You're a seasoned player in the game. And the only reason you came to me is because, for the first time in your life, you're up against someone who is just as strong or stronger and just as ruthless— the man you were always eager to get at but never knew how it would feel or what it would take. However, I need you to keep in mind the pros and cons of this whole entire thing. Your disadvantage here is your love for your enemy's daughter and your anger; this is the reason he is winning thus far. Your advantage is the fact that you're much younger, quicker, and most of all you have purpose. You have reasons to kill this motherfucker and believe you me son it hurts me every day that I haven't avenged your mother's death and that I'm not out there with you in a time like this. So, look at me. You make sure you do what you have to do to make sure your mother finally rest in peace, I don't want to see you again unless you have the news I want to hear. Guard! I'm ready!

I looked on as Polo walked away without looking back. It felt good seeing him; this visit was needed. I actually feel like I know what needs to be done. This war was by far the most serious of street shit I've ever been through, and shit is getting more real by the day, and I must defend my mother's legacy with every breath in my body, ain't no other way.

When I got back to the car, I called Biggs three times and sent a text but got nothing I tried calling bae phone to tell her I'm gone need her to go back with her dad. I was actually going to create an argument so that she would leave because the responsibility of protecting her is a great distraction. But then my phone rang it was a blocked call. I picked up thinking it may have been Polo, but instead I heard heavy breathing then a loud scream, a familiar scream and right then I knew the ball was out of my hand again, damn!

I hoped back in my rental and rushed to the airport. I had to think about what just happened. I'm no fool, and there is only one person that would need her to get to me, and that was Money. When I thought of this, I knew then that Money would not hurt his own child. However, I'm sure he is using the love I have for her to lure me in. She might not even be aware that it's her father who had her captured. I smiled to myself thinking that Money a lot easier made things for me, and instead of going back to Atlanta right away, I decided to go see my cousin Big Ducky in Brooklyn New York. He owed me a hundred favors, and on top of it all, he's a real shooter. I needed a motherfucker that's gone ride all the way, and most of all someone that I can trust. I know cuz is the right man for the job. I hoped on the next jet to the big apple.

SERENITY

*T*ears streamed down my face as I heard Jah's voice when he
answered. I was bound and gagged, not to mention pissy as
fuck. I was so fucking scared riding in that fucking truck that I pissed
everywhere. Besides being scared, I was in shock as I stared into the
eyes of my kidnappers. It was one thing to see Domo standing over
me, but to see Moniece was another. I knew she didn't like Jah, but
damn did she have to do all of this. I was kicking myself in the ass for
not listening to Jah. He told me not to trust anyone with my whereabouts, but my hard headed ass just had to tell Moniece. Now, look at
my dumb ass being held captive by this bitch and this crazy motherfucker who basically watched me grow up.

"I never thought I would see the day you went against your pops,
for a bitch ass nigga like Monsta at that. This is what happens when
you go against the grain. Beat that bitch's ass!"

Moniece came over to where I was and knocked me out of the
chair. I banged my head against the concrete floor, and I immediately
felt dizzy. My eyes got wide as I observe her bring down her foot on
me. There was nothing I could do as she started to hit, kick, and
punch me because I was still tied to the chair.

"Is he worth all of this, bitch?" she screamed in my face and quickly yanked the bandanna from around my mouth.

"Why are you doing this, Moniece? I thought you were my friend." I begin to choke on my own blood. I knew all that kicking to my chest and abdomen caused some internal bleeding.

"Fuck a friend! You're a naïve ass bitch! I'm about my mother-fucking money. My baby Domo deserves to be at the top, but your bitch ass daddy and your nigga got to go. So, they both need to pay if they want to see your ass alive again!"

"Shut the fuck up! I'm running this shit. I never told you to start running off at the fucking mouth. Get the fuck upstairs and cook a nigga something to eat." Moniece hauled ass getting up the stairs. I closed my eyes as tight as I could to keep from making eye contact with him.

"My nigga, Money! What it do my nigga. I got something you want, and it'll only cost you ten million to get it back." As I laid on the floor, I could hear the sound of my father's voice booming through the phone.

"Daddyyyy!" I screamed but was quickly silenced by a vicious kick to the back of the head.

* * *

MY EYES FLUTTERED as I tried to focus them. It was hard to see because my head was hurting and the sun from outside was shining in my face. After a minute or so of struggling to see, I locked eyes with Moniece.

"It's about time you woke up, princess." She was sitting back in a chair smoking a blunt.

"Why are you doing this? I thought we were friends."

"We are friends Serenity, but the love I have for my man trumps our friendship. You see you grew up in the lap of luxury over there in that big ass mansion. All you had to do was go to school, and your father handed you shit on a platter. Me, on the other hand, I had to allow my father to do sick shit to me so that I could get a decent meal. You see I had to get it out the mud. I had to do what the fuck I had to do to survive. Even at work, I'm sucking the human resources manager's dick just to add extra hours to my check. Life must be good living without worries. Pretty soon I won't have a worry or a care in the world. Domo's gone get this bread from them niggas Money and Monsta. "

I looked at her in pity. This bitch was truly delusional if she thought her riding for Domo was going to make him wife her or some shit. Her ass was nothing but a pawn in his sick ass game.

"I'm sorry that you have had to go through all of this, but it's not my fault that I have a father who loves me. You're sitting here talking about how your man trumped me, but that nigga is using you, Moniece."

"Girl, please! The only one around here being used is your dumb ass. Monsta was using you to get to your father. That dick must be really good since it caused you to turn your back on the one man who has loved you all of your life. I know it's killing your soul to be here tied up and that nigga is out fucking on the next bitch. You should have listened to me when I told you to leave his alone. Then again I'm happy you didn't because you led my nigga right to his ass."

The sound of commotion going on upstairs made her jump up and run out of the room. The next thing I heard was gunshots and the sound of heavy feet coming down the stairs. *Jah had come and rescued me,* I thought to myself. The tears of joy subsided seeing my father walking towards me with his gun out. In a way, I wanted it to be Jah, but I was happy as hell to get the fuck away from Moniece and Domo.

"See what happens when you don't listen to your father."

"Daddy I—"

"Shhhh! Don't say anything. Let me take you home where you belong."

My father removed the zip ties from my hands and lifted me up. All I could do was cry on his shoulder. So many emotions were going on inside of me. At the moment, I was happy as fuck to be out of danger. There was that lingering question that I needed to know, though. *Where was Jah and why hadn't he come for me?* It would kill my soul if he proved everybody right about using me.

MONEY

*T*he love I have so deep in my heart for Serenity wouldn't even allow me to kill her, even though she had been disloyal to me. The fact that she left my home and ran straight to the nigga Monsta let me know that she loved him. Just thinking about her loving that motherfucker made me think of her scandalous ass mother. I swear women will die trying to be in love with a nigga. Besides the anguish I was feeling about Serenity, I was pissed at this nigga Domo. After years of being my right-hand man, he had grown greedy. You see a nigga like me always two steps ahead of every nigga with a motive.

Domo had begun to move with jealousy in his eyes. I picked up on the shit, and I immediately put eyes on him. I don't understand where the fuck the greed came from because I've always made sure he and his family ate. Greed will make a nigga sign his own fucking death certificate. The moment he came up with the bright idea to touch Serenity, he had sealed his fate.

"Pleassseeeee don't do this!" Moniece screamed.

That shit went on deaf ears as I cut each of her fingers off with a pair of lawn shears. One by one I snatched them bitches off with satisfaction. This bitch was supposed to be a friend but let this silly ass nigga Domo get in her head. The stupid ass nigga has a family at home — a wife and six kids. Too bad I now have to off his ass. I'll make sure to give her something nice for the funeral.

"You good, babe?" my bitch Jazz asked as she handed me a bottle of Patrón. She had been on my team for years and one of my most loyal enforcers.

She enjoys killing motherfuckers just like I do. I guess that's why we've clicked so good. I've basically moved her into my home and was slowly moving Kee-Baby out. That ship has sailed. I've grown tired of her nagging ass. I need a bitch that's going to listen, not to mention a ride or die chick. Jazz was the total package. A bad bitch that toted guns and rode the dick like a pro. That's the type of bitch I needed on my team. Kee-Baby was still a little ass girl in my eyes. I needed a grown ass bitch that listened

"I'm not good. Do something to make me feel better." Jazz walked over to me and slipped her tongue into my mouth before grabbing a blow torch from the table. She walked over to Moniece and burned her face until it melted completely off.

I kicked my feet up on the table and flamed up a blunt. My dick got hard watching her perform real bitch duties. As I exhaled, I look up at Domo's bloody body hanging from the ceiling. He was knocked out cold and barely alive. My men had beaten him within inches of his life. I needed to be the last thing he laid eyes on before he checked out. The more I got high, the more sick shit came to my mind.

"Serenity, come down to the basement," I spoke through the intercom. Moments later she strolled in looking like a love sick puppy. It angered me to see my daughter fucked up over a nigga. No father ever wants that for his daughter.

"Yes."

"Come down the stairs there's something I want you to do." She was standing at the top of the stairs afraid to come down. I reached my hand out to her and grabbed her hand. She slowly walked down the stairs but quickly tried to run back up. I quickly grabbed her and led her over to where Moniece's body was at.

"I don't want to see this, Daddy!"

"You need to see this, Serenity. This is what the fuck happens when a motherfucker crosses me or fucks with someone I love. Growing up I shielded you from this part of me, and that's why you fell in love with that bitch ass nigga that paid attention to you. You were kept away from the streets, and that's why you have no street smarts. A chick with street smarts would have known Jah's intentions from the jump. We'll handle that situation later. Right now, I want you to end this motherfucker's life for fucking with you."

She started to shake her head no as I forced my gun in her hand. She was shaking like a leaf, and it pissed me off.

"Grab the gun Serenity and show that bitch ass nigga you not to be played with," Jazz coached.

"Nooo! Please don't make me do this!"

Her crying pissed me off to the point where I snatched the gun and emptied the clip inside of Domo. The nigga didn't have an inch of fight in him. I was actually tired of looking at his snake ass. To give a nigga the shirt off your back and they turn around and betray you will fuck the hardest of niggas up. I was glad I was rid of his ass. Now I needed to focus on getting at this nigga Monsta.

MONSTA

ruth be told it's been almost a week now that I've been in New York and not knowing if baby girl was ok was really starting to eat at my conscience. After that call, there was never another follow-up call for ransom or instructions to lead me into a trap. The unknown of her well-being had me fucked up in the head, yet I've been waiting for a call, a text, or something to let me know she was ok. During that time, I've been losing my fucking mind. I hate the unknown. I had to hip Big Ducky to what's happening on my end, and of course, he was down.

I wasn't surprised when he told me that he needed me to help him put in some work on some shit he couldn't afford to leave unhandled. Big Ducky was a real street nigga and the true definition of it. He was a heavy set nigga with a low cut Caesar and a goatee. He was a true Brooklyn nigga; in other words, he is as cruddy as they come. I was standing on the curve of Marcy Avenue when Big Ducky pulled his 2017 GMC Denali up so close on the curve I had to take a step back almost spilling my coffee all over my Fendi fit.

I jumped inside the truck and noticed Ducky had at least thirty thousand dollars in the middle console with a .45 caliber hand gun on his lap. Right after he dapped me up and passed me the blunt, he had a call on one of his many phones. Due to his facial expression, it was obvious the news he was getting on the other end of the phone wasn't good at all.

He slammed the phone down and whipped the extra-large SUV in the middle of the busy street. I held on the best as I can as he maneuvered through the streets of New York at top speed, all while smoking a blunt. I know he a convicted felon probably on his last strike but yet there is at least three to four guns with a large amount of money— the total recipe for a complete fuck up, but I guess niggas like Ducky don't see past the moment. They're true knucklehead always on go mode, with no kind of brain whatsoever and sometimes as sad as it is to say, in these streets you need niggas like Big Ducky. Truth be told chess won't be chess without pawns.

Cuz pulled the extra-large SUV to a sudden halt in front of the Fort Green projects building. He cocked his gun and jumped out the vehicle. I followed him hoping that he doesn't do anything that can cost me my life. God knows I already got too much on my plate as it is already.

We walked into a large crowd where a group of girls was fighting like they were getting paid for it. One of the girls was hitting the other girl who was beating another girl ass with a bat. Then before I blinked, Big Ducky shot the girl with the bat, grabbed the other girl by her hair, and then hit her with the butt of the gun in her face. He then picked up the girl they were jumping in his arms and drug her back to the car while the crowd ran and surrounded the bleeding girl Ducky just shot.

I had to ask what the fuck was going on and he told me this was his dead brother Fat Dog's daughter and he ain't gone let nobody play with her. I shook my head and started praying the entire ride back to the house. This was the bullshit I didn't need right now. I told cuz we had to handle that shit he needed help with and get back to Atlanta ASAP. He passed me the blunt and said, "Say no more."

* * *

A FEW HOURS LATER, Ducky and I sat in the back seat of a cab suited and booted. I followed his lead when he got out the car and walked into the bodega on the corner of a busy street. *This was some wild shit,* is all I could think to myself. I needed Ducky, so I had to be extra careful that he doesn't get fucked up before we get back on the road.

When we walked into the little narrow store, cuz walked right to the back of the store, opened a door, and walked down some steep stairs. When we got to the bottom, there were like six women in thongs and no top bagging up heroin, while another counted the money and placed it in a neat pile. When Ducky saw this, his eyes narrowed with anger. He pulled the twelve gage shot gun from his bag and started smoking everything that was breathing.

I had to hit two of the Spanish niggas who came from the rear end in the head to stop them in their tracks. Ducky told me to grab the money. I scraped it all off the table and into the bag. He never touched the dope. When we got back into the car, I had to ask him what type of shit was that. He told me some Dominican niggas had hit his people's block in Harlem. He explained that he owed his African connect a favor. He didn't explain much more, and I didn't need him too, I just needed to get back in route to Atlanta, to cancel this nigga Money once and for all.

When we got back to Big Ducky's crib, he handed me two large stacks of money. I could tell it was like forty or fifty bands, which was not bad. When I took the money, he said, "That's half of what I owe you, and depending on what type of shit you get me into down in that country ass shit, we may be able to call it even, cuzzo!"

* * *

HOURS LATER, we were on the road heading south. As Ducky drive and "Southern Smoke" came through the speakers, I felt my eye lids started to become heavy. Then without warning, I was a kid again.

"I hate you, Money! I fucking hate you! You're leaving me for that bitch! My rent is past due and you out here fucking this boney bitch! Fuck you, hoe!

"What the fuck nigga, you aight? You're gonna have to lay off the chronic, cuzzo. This bud is too heavy for you country niggas. You went to sleep and it looked like you were fighting in your dreams."

"Man, fuck that and pass the blunt."

I didn't feel it was needed to tell my cuz that I be having dreams of the day my mother died in front of me. That's my demon, and I deal with it the best way I can— sometimes I can control it and sometimes I can't.

VBBRR...

"Hello! Hello! You left my daughter for dead young man. She was kidnapped under your care, which only proves that you're not whom you say you are, or at least whom you think you are. It will behoove you to leave Atlanta because it's not safe here for you. Jah, my daughter, is off limits I will say this only once..."

CLICK!

"Fuck you! Fuck you!" I slammed my phone down on the dashboard, cracking the screen along with the dashboard.

Big Ducky passed me the blunt in silence and pressed down harder on the gas. "We only got to get through the Carolinas and we there, cuz. Just a few more hours and we there, word!"

I hate that I fell for Serenity. I hate that I love this woman because if I didn't, it would have made killing this motherfucker a lot easier. I thought he was behind her kidnapping the entire time and God knows if he wasn't. I guess now he appears to be the one that has her best interest, and only God knows what kind of lies he filled her head with. The unknown is beginning to haunt me, and right now, I know it would be in my best interest to exercise the one fucking thing I do not have, which is patience. Whoever it was that kidnapped Serenity knew Money, and Money knew them. That's why it was so easy for him to go get her and make it look like I fucking abandon her. This motherfucker was so slick and conniving, but in these streets ain't no rules.

I tried calling Serenity number, but he obviously made her change it. So the entire time I thought Money had her to try to bait me in, he actually made someone kidnapped her just to make it look like he is the true fucking hero and I have no interest in her well-being. That shit is eating at me the most. In that case, if I knew better, I would have never left for New York, but as I know, everything is preordained. And because of this law, I know that everything that is happening is happening for a reason.

I just have to use this time to exercise patience and plan this shit out all the way to the end. I didn't see this coming at all. I didn't see that he would make it to where Serenity would despise me, but I understand that he had to do so only because if his daughter is in love with me, it gives me leverage to get at him. Of course, he couldn't afford that because I'm sure he never believed that I actually cared for her. At times, it's hard to fucking believe she is even his child to be real about it.

The one thing that's eating me away is the fact that he would dictate his own child's life with deceit. This motherfucker deserves everything I got coming for him. Honestly, I wish I had known Serenity was his daughter before feelings got involved because this shit wouldn't have even gotten this far. My mind was running a million miles per second. The more I think, the angrier I become, so I decided on just sleeping this shit off because it was out of my control for now— just for now.

Big Ducky looked at me then back at the road. He then said to me in a low and grim tone, "Cuz, let me tell you something. You may be older than me and all, but we both know once you become emotional, you lose your true train of thought, which can cost you your life or freedom. The good thing about everything here is we at least know where she is. I understand how you feel. I don't know how you feel but trust me I understand, and I'm here with you.

I got a partner from Chicago that's in the A that can be of some use for us. Right now you're down cuzzo, and you need to get back up. So, every move has to be calculated and done with precision. There ain't no time to get angry and shit. That's what he tried to do with that phone call— get up under your skin cuz, but right now the name of the game is patience."

SERENITY

*I*t had been a month since I was kidnapped and the last time I saw Jah. I was going crazy overthinking things. A part of me wanted to believe that he had been hurt or worse— dead. It was crazy that I wished he was dead because then I wouldn't feel so stupid. In my heart, I knew that he had left me hanging. I didn't want to believe for a minute that Jah had left me to die. If there was one thing about him, it was that in his arms, I felt safe. So, it's crushing me that he never even reached for me. I just keep having flashbacks of different intimate moments with us. He made the shit feel so real, but in reality, it was all fake. I've sunk into a deep depression because I simply can't cope with his actions. That added with the fact that I was again stuck at my father's house. I'm grateful that he rescued me, but it's the last place I want to be.

He hasn't given me an inkling that he will hurt me for betraying him. However, I feel uncomfortable in his presence. There's something about the way he looked at me that makes me uneasy. It's like his mocking me or laughing at my pain. He's saying, "I told your dumb ass" without actually saying it. I had been dreading having a much-needed conversation with him. Despite everything that happened at the end of the day, he's my father, and I owe him an explanation.

My palms sweated as I stood outside of my father's office door. After blowing out the breath that I was holding in, I gained the courage to knock on the door.

"Hey Daddy, it's me. Can I come in?"

"Yeah!" His voice boomed, and I damn near wanted to walk the fuck away.

His door swung open, and he stepped to the side so that I could come in. I walked over and sat down in the chair in front of his desk. Once he took his seat, he stared at me for a minute. I watched his guys glance down at numerous pictures on his desk. It piqued my interest, so I slightly leaned over. Call me crazy but I could have sworn I saw a picture of Jah. My father quickly closed the folders and leaned back in his chair. He lit his cigar and puffed off it a couple of times before speaking.

"Talk to your old man. It's been a long time since we talked to one another. Why do you think that is?"

"Look, Daddy. I understand that you're upset with me about dealing with Jah, but I swear to you my love for you has never changed. I'm sorry that I left and didn't say anything, but you left me no choice. I'm a grown woman, and you were treating me like a child telling me who I could and could not be with. Daddy, you had no right to tell me I couldn't be with Jah. I love him!"

I knew I wasn't supposed to say that last part, but I got carried away. I couldn't even believe that I had said it out loud. For so long I had been in denial about the way I felt about him. My ass must have really had it bad for Jah to say that shit to my father.

"How dare you sit in front of me spewing so much fucking disrespect? Where in the fuck did you get your heart from? Never mind, I already know you get that shit from your weak ass momma. You love a nigga who couldn't even come and save your fucking life when you were in danger. I told you from the jump he was only using your ass to get back to me. Now, look at you sitting here looking stupid over a nigga that don't give a fuck about you. Is this the bitch ass nigga you love?"

He threw the folder across the table at me and all of the photos fell in my lap. I thumbed through the numerous photos of Jah with other women. I cringed looking at the photos of one woman in particular. There were pictures of her and Jah fucking on the balcony of his condo. I couldn't bear to look at them anymore, so I threw them on the floor. I sat there in silence trying not to cry in front of my father. The last thing he needed to see was me crying over that deceitful ass nigga. Instead, I tucked my tail between my legs and gave him the satisfaction he wanted.

"I just wanted to tell you that I was sorry for disrespecting you. If I hurt you, it was never my intention. I now know that you did it to protect me." He stood from his seat, walked over, and kissed me on the forehead.

"I love you more than you know, Serenity. I do this because I want what's best for you. If you ever decide to lay up with my enemy again, the outcome will not be happy for you. I take loyalty very seriously, especially when its family. Here's some money. Security will take you over to Kee-Baby's shop to get you ready for tonight. We have a very important dinner we've been invited to by an associate of mines. It would do you good to get out of this house and get back to the Serenity I know. The car will be here to pick you up at eight tonight. Don't be late."

* * *

I SAT in the backseat of Lincoln Navigator in deep thought. I was trying my best not to lock eyes with the guy who was driving me. He looked so fucking creepy. It's probably just my nerves. I swear after Domo kidnapped my ass, I don't trust a fucking soul. My father had me so irritated because he wouldn't allow me to wear the dress that I picked out. He insisted I rock a Givenchy off the shoulder evening gown with a pair of studded Louboutin's, not to mention the massive amount of diamonds I was rocking. He was going all out for whoever was throwing this party. I couldn't wait to see who it was. It was probably nothing but a damn drug distributor. That's the only time he goes all out like this.

About an hour or so later, the driver was finally pulling into one of the most gorgeous estates I had ever seen. He helped me out of the truck, and I couldn't help but marvel at the exterior. It was all white and gold. A beautiful fountain sat in the middle of the winding driveway. There were rose bushes spread out all over the front lawn. There were numerous luxurious cars parked in the driveway. I became more and more curious about whose house it was and why in the hell my father wanted me here.

As I walked up to the door, it swung open, and I swear my heart skipped a beat. It had to be a dream and a complete nightmare. It was impossible that this person was standing in front of me. I looked around waiting for somebody to say this shit was a joke. There was no way Chino was standing in front of me. He was supposed to have life in prison. He was my first everything, and we had plans to be married and live happily ever after, but that all changed when he got caught trafficking drugs for my father.

The day they sentenced him to life was the day my life changed forever. That morning before his sentencing, I found out that I was pregnant with his baby. I couldn't bring myself to tell my father. So Kee-Baby and me came up with traveling to France. Of course, he didn't care because we wouldn't be home getting on his nerves. We ended up staying in France for the duration of the pregnancy. Kee found a loving family to take my son. I literally didn't want a baby at that time. I've held this secret in for so long that I made myself forget about it, but standing in front of him makes me remember everything. Even the love we shared.

"Don't act like you don't miss a nigga. It's been seven years my love. No phone calls, no visits, no money on the books, or no letters. It's okay no need to explain why you didn't reach for a nigga. All is forgiven. Come inside I have someone I want you to meet. Baby C come over here! I want you to meet someone." He sipped from his champagne glass and winked at me. In the distance,

I observed my daddy and Kee-Baby talking and playing with the little boy.

"Huh, Daddy!"

My eyes bulged looking down at the little boy. I covered my mouth in shock staring at the tiny birthmark that sat on his right cheek just like my mother had.

"Say hello to your mother." Before I could say anything, I fainted.

* * *

"WAKE UP, SERENITY." A slight smack to both sides of my face made my eyes flutter. I looked up at Kee-Baby. I was wide-awake now and filled with rage. I quickly sat up and looked around the unfamiliar, but luxurious room that I was in.

"Get your fucking hands off of me! How could you do this to me?" I lost my composure, and I started fucking her up. One look at her sent me into a rage like no other. I couldn't believe she had betrayed me.

"Stop it right now!" my father's powerful voice boomed as he snatched me off of her like a rag doll.

"I trusted you, Kee! Why? Pleaseee! Just tell me why you didn't keep your word," I cried.

"I'm sorry, Serenity. Your father knew all along. I couldn't go against him. Please forgive me!"

"Why would you have me walking around thinking I had given my son up for adoption when you guys have had him all along?

"No I had him all along," Chino added as he stepped into the room and walked closer to me.

I stepped back because I didn't trust him, my father, or Kee. All of these motherfuckers were snakes. Come to think of it, everybody in my life is some damn snakes. What did I ever do to deserve this shit?

"How is that possible, Chino? Last time I checked your ass was in Federal prison serving life."

"Had you cared you would have known that the shit was over-turned on a technicality. I've been home for seven years building my own empire. It was only right I give my first born son the opportunity to have everything you tried to take away from him."

"It wasn't like that. I didn't want my father to know, and I was in no condition to raise a baby on my own. He didn't deserve to be raised looking at his father behind glass. I refused to bring my son to a fucking prison every week. I'm sorry, but that's not the life I wanted."

"It's okay, Serenity. All is forgiven. That's why we brought you here. This is your party." My father walked towards me and pulled me into his embrace. I pushed his ass up off of me.

"My party?"

"Yes, this is your welcome home party. Our son is here with me, and this is where you belong. I had this estate built from the ground up just for you. Get comfortable and get used to it. Your home is here with your family."

Chino stepped in front of my father and kissed me on the lips. I quickly tried to run the hell out of the room, but the door opened and in walked my son. He wrapped his arms around my waist. I couldn't leave him even if I wanted to.

BIG DUCKY WILLIAMS

*S*ince I got to Atlanta, shit has been crazy. Being here while cuz is going through it like this made it obvious how real shit is and is about to get. I always looked up to Monsta. He was always the cousin from the south that everybody loved to be around. I remembered back in the days we couldn't wait until he arrived for the summer. Shit changed up quick when his momma got killed. We've always been close as fuck though, so it was mandatory we kept in touch. I would always over hear stories about him while growing up by other family members, especially at Big Momma's house on Sundays.

By the time I was in high school, his name was already ringing bells in the streets. A lot of mother fuckers judge him because of his cut throat mentality, but truth be told the nigga did witness his mother's death. Shit like that would fuck with anybody's head, no doubt. Cuz ended up being another statistic, a true product of his environment. Life was never the same after his mother's death.

Sitting on the bench at my homeboy from Chicago Taz's backyard overlooking a man-made lake, this shit had me in a vibe. The scenery alone brings forth peace and comfort.

It's fucked up I'm not out here on some vacation type shit, but its fam and at the end of the day, ain't no gangsta is a gangsta unless he is there for his family when they need him the most. Every time I needed that nigga Monsta, he came through without excuse. I had to smile when I thought about that time I owed some Africans fifty large for fucking up some heroin they had fronted to me. I didn't have the time at the time to be beefing with a bunch of Zulu tribe, mother fuckers, so I called cuz not sure if he had that type of bread. When I tried to tell him about the situation, he cut me off and told me to tell him how much. I gave him the exact amount needed, and three days later, a bad thick red bitch knocked at my door holding a black Adidas gym bag with seventy-five thousand cash in it. I text him that I only needed fifty. He texted me back that if I needed fifty to get out the hole once that bill is paid, I'd still be on my dick, so he told me to keep the extra and that the bitch was on him. By the time my phone was back in my pocket, the lil' piece was already butt ass naked walking back into the room. Damn, just thinking bout that bitch had my dick hard. *I wonder if he still got that bitch's math, yo!*

Shawty's ass was so fat and soft it was like a big bag of water. She squatted in front of me, took 'Frank the Plank' out my pants, and made Karrine Steffans look like a joke. Even while giving Frank the business, she was making that big motherfucker wobble back and forth while she choked herself with the rod of correction. The bitch was as freaky as a bowl of worms, and she had that sloppy toppy for real, for real— the type of shit that would have had a nigga wifing the lil' bitch of the head game alone.

I couldn't take that shit any longer. She had the tip of my dick sensitive like a soft ass nigga. I know she had to think I was a weak or some shit with how fast she had a nigga busting. And the fucked up part about the entire shit was as soon as I bust, all that moaning and shit she was doing stop immediately, I mean fucking abruptly. She had a nigga second-guessing my own dick game and shit. She got dress and left without saying shit else. It wasn't my fault she had all that good shit between them ham hocks. Damn, I'd like to get a piece of that pussy again. On God, you hear me.

I looked at the blunt I was smoking and wasn't impressed and decided whenever all this shit blows over I'm most definitely coming back to flood the streets with some real piff; this shit wasn't hitting on nothing. I heard some movement behind me. When I looked around, I saw it was cuz pulling up a seat by the pool. Man, that nigga look down bad, yo! This shit is some heavy shit from what he hit me with, but only the God's know how deep this shit really is. However, I have no fear because we bout to roll on these motherfuckers like an avalanche in a minute.

Right now, like I told cuz, the name of the game is patience, and we got to power all the way up. From what he explained to me and from what I've seen thus far, this old head Money is a bad mother-fucker. And, from the looks of it, the nigga has mad influence over the city. Since it's been that way for over twenty years, the only way to nip this shit is to knock that nigga head off his motherfucking neck, and you better believe I'm gone be there when that motherfucker hits the floor.

I don't know the history of him and the broad, but she saved my nigga's life, so I can see why he is all fucked up about her and what not!

I don't go asking him his personal business and shit, I ain't never been that type of nigga, but on some real shit, I hate seeing cuz this weak. Looking at him, I can tell this shit is way too heavy for just him to carry, and that's why we here. I looked at my flesh and blood, and right then, I knew if I had to I'd lay it down for my cuz. What's fucking me is how he fell in love with the daughter of the nigga who killed his moms and his main man Dex, what are the odds in that? It's like the universe made them meet for a reason and time will expose the true purpose behind it all.

I have to find a way to help my cuz bounce back in the game and keep his head on the swivel. Everything moving forward has got to be tighter than fish pussy.

I flicked the roach from between my fingers, threw back the rest of the cognac I had in my glass, and then made my way over to my cuz. He never saw me approaching because he had his head held down. Due to his demeanor, I decided to give him some space.

MZ. LADY P AND CHIEF

"I know it's heavy on you cuz but keep your head up."

I never stopped to look to see if he took my advice nor did I wait for a response, I just kept it moving.

The only way to cheer up a real nigga is pussy, money, and weed. I had to check pussy off the list because right now no outsiders were allowed in due to how things were operating. Shit was really real, and one mistake may result in a fatality. The next best thing is money, and I know these country motherfuckers had that cash out here, so I decided to get lost in the city to see what type of shit I can get into and to get at the money. To be honest, I needed a rush myself. A lil' boost to the good old adrenaline pump always shakes a nigga's head back in the game.

I ended up in Buckhead. I passed the famous Phipps Plaza and then just up a few more stoplights. I saw a Rolex Store. I scoped it out for a few hours before I went into the store, only to find out this shit was as sweet as a fucking lollipop. It was a one way in, one way out type of set up.

Only one guard was present before you entered the store. There were no lock doors and then BOOM, fucking heaven on earth! There was nothing but crystal clear glasses filled with gold and platinum pieces ranging from twelve thousand to a hundred and ten thousand a piece. *This was the perfect lick,* I thought right before the slim, tall, happy go lucky motherfucker with the name tag that read "store manager Barry Johnson" walked up to me.

The dude looked like a viscous creep and a fucking flaming faggot. To be honest, I don't know why I was surprised. This was Atlanta after all.

I took some pictures on the slick of all the streets and surrounding buildings. I got back into this little as Tesler and pulled into a McDonald's parking lot to count how many cameras were in the area from the pictures I've taken. From where the McDonald's sat, I was able to record the intersection for fifteen minutes to see if the lights were consistent on how long they took to change form red to green. It was a three-minute window give or take forty seconds between each intersection. After I was done mapping out the area, I went back to the lab and broke everything down with Taz and Cuz— they were with the shits. We went over everything again for about another hour, before we left out in the Ram Dually to just verify everything and figure out what routes we were going to take to get away. Everything had to be planned to the end and executed as planned.

After everything had been finalized, cuz took us to his garage where he had some 007 shit going on. The nigga opened a fucking wall, and all type of weapons were on display. I looked at the nigga and shook my head I always knew cuz was on a different level shit, but this shit here nigga is some Bruce Willis action pack shit! This nigga had me like a kid in a fucking candy store. I saw him smile as he heard me talking shit. I knew my plan would help eventually because the law has never changed. It's been get the money and then the power— that's just the way this shit was designed period, and no matter what once you love yourself, you're gonna protect yourself. So, I knew once I could have gotten cuz to agree on the lick, it would have taken his mind off all that shit that was weighing him down. I knew he would have no choice but to focus and get all the way in the game because as we all know fuck ups right now are unacceptable.

Jah handed Taz and me a Spectre M4. He then handed us both two extra fully loaded clips and two suppressors. Opening one of the drawers, he took out some shit that looked like some new model hand grenades. He handed Taz and me one each as well as two paper weight bulletproof vests. We strapped 'em on then jumped into the bullet proof Jeep Wrangler he had parked around the back.

By the time we got back on the road, it was five a.m. We parked right across the street waiting for the manager to open the store. The store opens at eight a.m., and we were there at seven thirty. We definitely didn't want to miss the opportunity of getting in early where there weren't too many people in the store. An hour and a half later after listening to Steve Harvey speaking like the God of love, a black Mercedes E-320 pulled up into the parking lot. I tapped Taz on his shoulder and nodded my head in the direction of the luxury vehicle.

Taz placed the Jeep in gear and pulled up beside the Benz. The driver was too busy texting on his phone that he never saw when

Monsta jumped out the truck until his elbow went through the driver side of his car glass. This wasn't a part of the plan, so Taz and I were a bit puzzled, and all I could have hoped was that cuz was in his right state of mind. When we saw that he was walking dude into the store, we pulled our mask down and walked in behind covering the door.

"Take me to the back. I want the diamonds, certificates, and cash. Yo fam, start the clock! We got sixty seconds, move, move, move sixty seconds on the clock.

After Cuz had said what it was, he walked the scared, fragile manager to the back. By the time I stuffed the last Rolex into the bag, Monsta was already on the way out.

"Let's go!"

The best part about a robbery is getting away with it, jumping in the car and feeling your heart beat through your chest with your adrenaline pumping at a hundred and twenty miles per hour gives you that rush that makes you feel alive. Nevertheless, counting the profit is always the sweetest though.

Thirty minutes later, we pulled into a garage Monsta owned. I emptied my back pack first. We counted twenty-eight Rolexes and with the price tag stuck to each of them that alone added up to be two hundred forty thousand big faces. Taz's inventory tallied up to four hundred and sixty thousand. When Cuz opened his bag, it was fucking empty. The room grew silent as he then opened the small part of the bag and pulled out a blue velvet bag filled with IF— internally flawless— diamonds. I almost lost my motherfucking mind, word to God. Man, I was ready to tell that nigga fuck that bitch, and let's go buy a new bitch, then ball like Tracy McGrady.

Before this lick our pockets were comfortable. Well, I can't speak for Monsta, but Taz and my shit was straight before, but now we are some wealthy niggas, and I want to stay alive to spend this mother-fucker. I know! I know! The whole reason for hitting the lick was to get our money up because the opp was too heavy but damn, fuck what cuz is talking bout we going to Onyx tonight to fuck up a check, shit! I'm bout to go to war, and I'm not sure if we're gonna live or die, so tonight I'm gone definitely live.

MONSTA

A lot of fuck shit been going down lately. It's been months since I've heard from Serenity, I ain't never been the type of nigga to chase behind nan bitch when I don't even chase my liquor. I feel it in my stomach that Serenity needs me. I can't explain the feeling and to be honest I don't give a fuck what anyone thinks, I won't give up on her. Shit just won't feel right if I walked away.

I won't deny that I fell for her and fast, something I never do. But in all reality, if it wasn't for her I'll probably be dead, so for that, I would forever be loyal. It's fucked up that the nigga that took my momma from me is her father, but at the end of the day she will have to understand, and I'm pretty sure she would. Most women that love their father's normally at least have one picture of him in their house, but I don't remember seeing any of Money in her house, and if I did, I would remember.

I was down bad when I heard she got kidnapped and I wasn't able to do shit about it. I was in a place I wasn't familiar with within myself. I felt like I lost something close to me, a part of me. It's hard to truly explain with words, but just the thought of her dying because I wasn't able to be there for her really fucks with my mental every day. I often wonder if she is alive, hoping she is alive. It's like a thick guilt that's weighing down on me, and I know I would never be the same unless I can find her whether dead or alive at this point.

Looking at these diamonds in my hand, I now know that my dreams have been answered and I'm no longer street rich but wealthy. When Big Ducky put me up on the move, I wasn't into it at first, but then I remember a time I did a bid up the road and was bunked with an old head nigga who use to hit jewelry stores and shit. He would always say to me that diamonds are better than money, and if he was to ever get out of prison the first joint he would hit would be a Rolex store just for the diamonds because all their diamonds are IF and imported straight from Africa and Indonesia.

So when Big Ducky ran it by me at first, I was going to decline, because not only did I thought it was an ass backwards idea, but stores and shit have never been my MO, ya dig? Then it hit me like a truck doing a hundred and eighty miles per hour. It was like I could hear the old head's voice clear as day telling me to do it. I was in a funk because I felt defeated by the man that murdered the woman who pushed me out of her womb. Then on top of it all, the woman who saved my life needed me to save hers, and I wasn't able to do shit about it. My best friend is dead because of me, my lil' niggas died defending me, and it all started to weigh in on me and let's just say it's more than I can bear.

I know in order to knock Money's head off his motherfucking neck, I was going to have to step my game all the way the fuck up. That nigga had old long money, and the nigga's cash has been longer than train smoke since I was a jit, so it's nothing for a nigga like that to push out a couple grand to clean up some shit. I tried coming at him with heart, pressure, and everything I got, but I lost in ways no amount of money would ever be able to repay.

I realized I was sitting in my living room in complete darkness thinking maybe too deeply into things allowing my mind to play tricks on me. I decided to turn the television on to take my mind off of my vicious reality. Ironically, the words of Tony Montana came booming through my surround sound. "Manolo, you got it all wrong meng! Get the money, the power, and then everything falls into place."

KEELAH

I sat in the middle of my bed unsure of my future. Hell, I wasn't even sure about my present. After years of being with Money, I was completely fed up with his bullshit. I've been in love with this man since I was fifteen. There was never a time when I felt like I wouldn't love him anymore. These days he's making this shit harder and harder. The crazy thing about all of this was that I didn't ask for this life with him— it was given to me. He made it his business to make me comfortable because of the circumstances that surrounded me ending up with him. My father owed him money for a drug debt. Instead of him paying the money like a real father would, he gave me to him in exchange for his life.

When I first went to live with him, things were nothing like I expected. He had a daughter I was close in age with so that made it easier. At the same time, he let it be known that I was there to be his woman. In the beginning, he was never mean. He was actually loving, kind, and generous. I had access to more money than I had ever seen in my life. From the jump, I was spoiled rotten, and I wanted for nothing.

He never exposed me to the other part of his life, the life where he murdered senselessly and ran the streets with an iron fist. The naïve part of me fell in love with a façade because that's what he portrayed when he was around me. In front of me, he was the best man that a chick could ask for. At such a young age, I didn't realize what he was doing to me was a way to own me. After all of these years, I realize he does indeed own me.

One would think that as much as he's been whooping my ass lately, I would have been run away from him. As I sit looking around at the luxurious life that I love, all I can do is wonder am I willing to lose it all by walking away? I slightly turn my head to the left and catch a glance at my face. The fresh black eye and swollen nose made me cringe. I knew that I had to leave because Money was becoming meaner and more vicious. This beef with Monsta had him going crazy and taking the shit out on me, not to mention the fact that Serenity isn't fucking with either of us. I'm not mad at her because she has every right to be mad. I was supposed to be her friend, but Money had a hold on me that was out of this world.

I should never have betrayed her by giving Baby C to him. I should have given him to the family we initially chose. When Money got wind of what we were up to, he beat the fuck out of me. I couldn't take him burning me with cigarettes and hitting me with a wire hanger to get the truth out, so I had no choice but to tell him what was going on. All of this time I knew it would come back to haunt me. I just never imagined that Money would reveal the shit the way that he did. Over the years, I've learned so much about Money. He's evil and gives no fuck whom he hurts as long as he gets what he wants. I've watched him hurt his own daughter for his own selfish reasons. If he doesn't give a fuck about her, I know for a fact he doesn't give a fuck about me.

I love Money, but not enough to allow him to continue beating my ass, then turning around thinking money is going to change things.

I know that lying in bed won't help the situation. There was money to be made at the shop. Out of everything that Money gave me, I owned it out right. I still can't believe that he had put it in my name. After getting up and getting dressed, I got ready to head out of the house. As I walked down the long corridor of our home, I could hear the faint sound of moaning. My heart raced as I slowly walked towards where the sounds were coming from. As I stood outside of Money's man cave, I struggled with whether or not I should go inside. Either way, he was going to be mad so why the fuck not. I twisted the knob and went inside. I stood numb watching as he had the bitch Jazz bent over the theater seat fucking her doggy style. He was so into it that he never noticed I was standing in the doorway. She did, though. Before she could let him know that I was watching them, I got the fuck out of there. I wasn't mad or sad. I was numb and content at the same time. This old ass nigga truly didn't give a fuck. There I was a couple of rooms down, and he was having sex with another woman like this wasn't my house. Then again, it's not my house. All of this shit is his, and he can have it. I'm good. Fuck him.

* * *

"Can I get a quick lining, ma?"

I looked up from sweeping the shop up for the night. This nigga was huge standing over me with that deep ass voice. I was kicking my own ass for not locking the door. Shit, it was after business hours, and my feet were hurting. I had booked me a room, and I was ready to lay it down. There was no way I was going back to the house I shared with Money. I was exhausted physically and mentally. My ass just wanted to lay my tired ass down.

"I'm sorry, but I'm closed." I watched as he sat his ass down in the chair like I wasn't talking to him. I didn't have time for this. Against my better judgment, I dropped the broom and decided to give him a lining.

"Don't fuck my shit up. As you can see, I'm a handsome ass nigga, and the ladies love this beard. I need my shit on point."

I rolled my eyes at his rude ass as I wrapped the cape around him. I glanced at him in the mirror and noticed that he was kind of cute. He was staring at me a little too hard, and it was creeping me out.

"I'm a professional. Don't worry I got your extra rude ass."

"I'm not rude. I just say what I mean, and I mean what I say. By the way, I'm Big Ducky. What's your name, beautiful?"

"I'm Keelah." I grabbed my clippers and my small comb and began to trim him up. I couldn't help but take in the scent that he was wearing. It was so intoxicating."

"Keelah's a beautiful name for a beautiful woman."

I blushed but continued to cut his beard. I didn't want to look so excited about a simple compliment even though I was. I can't remember the last time I received a compliment from Money.

"Okay, you're all done." I brushed the hair off of him and removed the cape. He placed a one hundred dollar bill in my hand along with a business card.

"Keep the change and make sure you use the number on the card. All the makeup in the world won't cover that black eye you rocking. If you want to get away, I'm staying at Hilton on Peachtree. I'm just a phone call away, ma." He walked his big ole ass out like a boss.

The last thing I needed was to be trying to find comfort in another man. I was mainly interested because I had never been with any other man. Something inside of me said I needed to tear it up and throw it in the garbage. That needy part of me that longed for a man's affection made me put his business card in my purse. I didn't know when I was going to use it, but I knew that it would be soon.

SERENITY

It had been weeks and I was still trying to figure out this mommy thing. I never anticipated being a mother. If I had, I never would have given my son away in the first place. I haven't spoken to my father or Keelah since the night I found out everything. I was glad because I didn't have shit to say to either of them. I wish that I could just take my son, go far away with him, and never look back. Chino was refusing to let me leave his estate with my baby, so I was basically stuck trying to be a better mother to my son. I refused to leave him again. I had to tuck my tail between my legs and stay in his home. He wasn't holding me against my will, but I wasn't trying to leave my son.

Chino had actually been staying out of my way, and I was staying out of his. I just wanted to get to know my son, and so far, I had been doing a good job. It was so amazing how much he looked like both Chino and me. Never in a million years did I think we could make something so beautiful. Despite the circumstances of finding out about him, he's the best thing to come out of everything.

My mind had been so preoccupied with Baby C that I hadn't had much time to think of Jah. That was a good thing because it's the last thing I wanted to do. I missed him so much that it hurt. I went from lusting to loving him. Eventually, that love and lust turned to hate. How could he just leave me out in the cold like that? Then again, he was cold hearted. I should have expected that from him. As angry as I am with him, I can't help but to long for his touch.

Masturbating had become a daily thing for me. Even though my mind didn't want Jah, my pussy did. The pussy wanted who it wanted. Even though I couldn't have him in the physical sense, I could damn sure have him mentally.

* * *

"You know that I can help you with that, right?" The sound of Chino's voice made me jump. I quickly covered my body with the sheet. Embarrassed wasn't the word for how I was feeling. My ass was laid back with my Hitachi wand getting reading to cum. He fucked that shit up quick.

"I don't need your help. Next time you need to knock before coming in here."

"This is my motherfucking house, and I don't have to do anything. You're in here lusting over that bitch ass nigga, ain't you?"

I watched as his face turned into a mean scowl. He turned up a bottle of Avion Tequila and drank it straight down. This nigga was drunk.

"I didn't ask to be in this motherfucker. Let me get my mother-fucking son and bounce."

I jumped out of bed and was quickly met with a fist to my face. I was knocked back on the bed. My vision became blurry, and my head was banging. I was roughly pulled down to the edge of the bed. I tried to fight and move out of Chino's grip. I was disoriented but still aware of what was happening. He forcefully pulled my legs apart. The next thing I knew he was ramming his dick inside of me. It felt like I was being ripped in two.

"Your ass is never leaving this motherfucker with my son. I'll kill your ass first. Go ahead and cry for that nigga Jah. He doesn't hear you and he never will. I had my men kill his bitch ass. So, take this dick and get used to it."

I silently cried as he spoke and continued to rape me. He was telling me he had killed Jah, but I didn't believe him. My heart was telling me different. Jah would never allow my father or Chino to kill him, regardless of how he did me. He ain't no bitch ass nigga or a coward. It's going to take an army to kill him.

The more Chino thrust inside me, the more tears fell. I cried harder when I realized my son was standing in the door watching his father rape me. At that moment, I knew I had to get my son out of this situation. There was no way I could allow him to live with this sick motherfucker.

MONSTA

I needed to go back to my old spot for a few things; I wanted to be by myself. I needed time to think and digest everything that has recently transpired in my life. I waited until Taz and Big Ducky was knocked out then I made my move. I took an Uber to stay under the radar. As I drove through the city in the back seat staring out the window, I placed my ear buds to my iPhone 7 in my ear and pressed play to Kodak Black's new album. Driving through downtown Atlanta at night always helps free my mind and helps me think clearer. My mind was racing with memories of Serenity and plots of getting her back. When we pulled up to my old condo, I told my Uber driver to give me a few minutes while I ran upstairs.

When I got into my condo, I noticed a lot of shit was out of place immediately. I drew for my Springfield semi-automatic .45. I walked through my entire spot making sure it was clear. Once I was satisfied, I grabbed my passport, my jewelry, and some clothes. I dumped them into my red Versace gym bag and got the fuck out of there when I got back into the elevator. I felt a fucked up familiar feeling in the air. It was so thick I could've felt it in the bottom of my stomach.

When I walked out the double doors of the high rise, I saw my Uber Escalade truck parked in the same spot. I didn't pay attention to the two black Lincoln Navigators parked in front and behind my Uber. I looked behind me as I opened the back door to the truck and jumped in. When I got in, the doors locked immediately. I then noticed the driver behind the wheel was definitely not the mother-fucker that picked me up. I reached for my strap the same time the truck pulled off, and the lights behind me were beaming through the back window. I quickly looked back and noticed the same type of Navigator that was in front of us was behind of us along with my driver on the back mat bleeding from a bullet hole in the side of his head. *Damn,* is all I could of think to myself.

I fucked up majorly and underestimated my enemy, and if this is it, then I'm going out like Ox in *Belly*. They had me fucked up.

"If I was you, I would pay close attention to my surroundings. If we wanted you dead, you would be dead, so I wouldn't fuck that up. Sit the fuck back and enjoy the ride."

It took every bone and blood cell in my body to do as this fuck nigga told me to do, but he was right, so I had no choice but to let the shit play itself out.

About thirty minutes later, we pulled into this luxury driveway to a stone front house surrounded by beautiful trees and manicured lawn.

My door was opened, and there were three niggas behind me and three in front of me. The three in front of me turned around and started walking, which I took as an indication for me to follow. *They never search me, and I'm sure they knew I was strapped,* I silently thought to myself. I quickly glanced back. The three behind me was towing behind us only steps away. It then crossed my mind that I'm not even sure who the fuck these niggas were or belong to. Shit, with all the shit I've done and been into it could be anybody, but I'm sure it couldn't be Money, or else I would have already been dead. So, at this point, I took a deep breath and before I could exhale, I felt a sharp pinch in two areas of my back then my body went stiff as the mother fuckers behind me tased me. Darkness quickly covered me and then I was out. Fuck!

* * *

"WAKE THE FUCK UP! *Blap!*

When I came to, I could barely open my left eye. *Damn, I got caught slipping*, was the first thing that my mind registered. My lips were tight and swollen. The split in the middle of my lip was deep and bloody. As I slip my tongue across my lips, the burn began and from the feel of it, I'm sure I'm gone need stitches.

"Aggghh ooogh!" *Fuck.*

I hunched over as I tried to regain my breath. The old head Debo looking ass nigga just punched me in the stomach, knocking the fucking wind out of me. After I had got my breath back, I realized that I was hand cuffed to a chair.

"Look at you son; you're all fucked up! It would have pained your momma to witness what you have become. Normally a smart child would have learned from his mother's fuck up and would have gone to college and made something of themselves, but nah, you want to be a fucking hero. But nigga, you forgot one thing. This is real life, not some fucking Bruce Willis movie!

When he backhanded me, I fought with every bone in my body to break out of this mother-fucking chair. I'm sure I fractured my wrist in the process, but I felt like a fucking failure, having this nigga get at me twice. He had already took my mother and my best friend from me. Now he was trying to take Serenity. I felt like a fucking failure and at this point, I didn't give a fuck about living.

"I want you to see something son. See, I know you love my daughter, or that's at least what she believes. She definitely loves you and because the love for my baby girl is unconditional and it would pain her if my hand has your blood on it. So, I'm gone show you something. You deserve to know the truth because what I'm about to tell you I'm gone only gone say it once, so if I were you I would pay close fucking attention!"

I spat a pool of blood out on the floor next to his wingtip El Salvador Ferragamos. He smirked at me in pity and took a long pull on his thick cigar he turned his back on me in his glory. He reached for a remote, pressed a button, and a screen rolled down from the ceiling.

He looked back at me.

"Ready son?"

"Fuck you and I ain't your mother fucking son, pussy nigga!"

He laughed at my attempt to show that I'm ready to die on my feet and the last thing I'll ever do is give this fuck nigga the satisfaction of me crying or begging for mercy. He's got me bent, and if he knows what's good for his fuck ass, he will hurry up with it.

I looked as the room went black and the screen light up. At first, it looked like some type of ball mansion party or some shit, but then I saw Serenity hugging and being kissed by some pretty boy motherfucker.

I can't even flag that shit fucked me up. Then as I looked back up at the screen, I saw her dude and some lil' nigga who look just like them taking pictures and shit. The screen then pauses. Unconsciously I guess my head fell low.

"Pick your head up, son. I know what you're thinking and yes you're right; she has a family. She was supposed to be keeping an eye on you, but instead, she fell weak for your bullshit, fell in love with you, and forgot where she came from. But now, that she is back where she belongs I'm gone tell you this once and only once— stay the fuck away from Serenity! Do you hear me? *Blap!* Do you hear me you punk mother fucker!!? *Blap! Blap! Blap!* Do you fucking hear me, nigga? Get him the fuck out of here!"

* * *

"OH MY GOD! Somebody call an ambulance, Jesus, dude are you ok?"

"Get the fuck off of me!"

I know the bystanders that saw me get pushed out of a moving vehicle was concerned and only trying to help, but help was the last thing I needed. I asked the guy who was on the phone with the paramedics to let me explain my injuries to the dispatcher, and when he handed me the phone, I hung it up and quickly dialed Big Ducky number. I called twice and got the voicemail both times. I called the suite where we were staying because I didn't know Taz's number by heart. On the third ring, Taz deep voice grumbled through the phone. I told him where I was at and before I could get another word out, he said he was on his way.

About thirty minutes later, Taz pulled up to the curb where I was sitting, he jumped out the whip and assisted me into the passenger seat, the same time the ambulance and the police arrived. By the time they figured out that I was the bleeding victim, we were already pulling away from the curb.

Concerned I asked about Big Ducky, and Taz shrugged his shoulders notifying he wasn't too sure. He explained that he was knocked out up until I called, and when he went to wake Duck up and tell him what was happening, he wasn't there. Right before we got back to the hotel, Big Ducky called Taz's phone, and I could have heard him through the speaker asking for me in a concerned tone then quickly instructed Taz to meet him back at the hotel.

Minutes later, we were pulling up to the in front of the hotel. Taz helped me out the truck and assisted me up to the elevator and then to the room. Before Taz could have placed the key card in the door, Ducky bust the door opened with a wild look in his eyes. When he saw how badly beaten I was, he freaked the fuck out. I had to remind him to lower his voice and to calm down.

Taz rolled a blunt lit the tip then past it to me. I asked Ducky to help me out of my clothes, and those boys both assisted me. Right when I was putting my shirt over my head, I saw a lady with a familiar face staring at and my immediately when into investigation mode. I looked at her and already knew she the woman who obviously had Cuz out all night, but I kept telling myself I knew this bitch. Then it hit me like a ton of bricks.

"What's your name?" I asked with a heightened sense.

"Keelah." She spoke in a low tone

"Kee-Baby?"

"Yea, yea! Do I know you?"

"Nah bitch, but you're about to!" I tried to head towards her but Ducky stepped in front of me before I could make it over to her.

"Fuck going on Monsta?"

I heard how concerned Ducky was when he saw how things were going.

"That bitch is buddy's old lady."

"Who's buddy?"

"Money, that's his bitch, and she ain't leaving this motherfucker. Bolt her down, cuz."

"Cuzzo!! Are you sure man!"

"Fuck you mean if I'm sure nigga, don't be getting soft on me. That's her, now bolt the bitch down."

She stepped up to me and looked me in the eyes long and hard before she started slowly shaking her head.

"He is right; I am engaged to Money. Yes, that is true, but I'm no different from you Jah. I didn't have to come over here when I heard your family mentioned your name, but I'm familiar with your name because that's the name Serenity would mention all day every day. But, let me make myself clear. When it comes to Money, I'm no fucking different than you, and actually, I'm worst off than you because I'm a prisoner of his world. So, you can bolt me down, tie me down, keep me down, and guess what, Jah? I don't give a fuck because as long as I'm away from him is all my heart desires, so you're doing me a favor, but if you're willing to listen, I can help you. The reason he keeps getting the best of you is because he is using your pain and anger against you, so if you want my help I'll be more than willing to help you, but enough with the disrespect."

"Where is Serenity?"

"Right now, luv, the only way to get her back is through him and that nigga Chino. Money loves Chino like a son, and he is the only guy he sees fit to be with Serenity. So with Chino's money and power combined with Money's, it's gone take a lot to penetrate them."

"Where is she? Is she ok?"

"Hun, you look defeated, and I'm gone tell you this the best way that I could and straight up. Right now, Serenity needs to be the last thing on your mind. They will make sure nothing happens to her. I can assure you that, and she has her plate full with everything that is taken place in her life right now. So, if I were you, I would worry more about Money and Chino's next move and whatever you do instead of using rage and anger to guide you think out a plan to the end and execute it. You now have me on the inside, and in time when I can get to Serenity, I would share with her your love. For now get yourself some rest and if I was you, I wouldn't worry about going head to head with Money not just because he is a well-established guy, and you'd be giving him the reaction that he would be expecting. I'll be in touch with you, get better, and if I was you guys, I'd get out of this hotel. I'm sure he already knows where y'all are at."

After she had said her peace she placed her oversized shades back over her beautiful green eyes. Followed by placing a scarf over her head in an attempt to disguise herself. She left without looking back or saying another word. When the door closed behind her, I felt unsure, and I felt like the bitch finessed me out of holding her fuckin' ass hostage. But, I couldn't deny that she spoke some real shit, and at this point, all I could do is keep the faith and wait for her to prove herself real or fake.

I looked at Big Ducky who was deep in thought, and I told him don't stress it because he didn't know. Nevertheless, just the fact that we were at war and he all laid up with some random pussy was suspect, and I figured he was looking at how his weakness almost jeopardized our lives. Right now wasn't the time to be pointing fingers and playing the blame game, though. Ducky was my nigga and blood. He fucked up, but I know he would never do anything to purposely to get us caught up. As long as he saw where he fucked up, that's what holds merit with me.

TAZ

*C*oming from Chicago, I had seen a lot of shit and not too much surprises me, but this shit with Big Ducky and his cousin is real heavy. I swear I'm in an action movie fucking with these niggas. Ducky is my nigga though and the nigga Monsta seems like a standup guy and seeing everything that fool was going through, I know he need all the help he can get.

I made a call to my mans from the Virgin Islands. Lito was a nigga I met in Vegas. The nigga had long ass dreads. He was a simple looking guy, but his wrist was lit up like a chandelier, and he had more money on the craps table than everybody who was playing that night. We became kool and just kept in contact. A few years back, he had a problem on the west side of Chicago, and he called on me for a favor. I delivered, and a week later I had twenty-five bricks at my front door.

Right now the name of the game is to power up. The dude fam is beefing with obviously has the ups because his paper is longer and his team is stronger. Now, I've overheard about some other dude name Chino, so I know this shit is about to get wild, and I got six kids to live for. I ain't no coward, but I ain't no brave fool. I'm not gone jump ship when my mans need me the most, but I know right now they minds

MZ. LADY P AND CHIEF

are a bit blurred with all that's happening. So, I have to be the one with the level head and get us back in the game to get the job done so we can get home to our families.

I knew Monsta had come up on them diamonds and he wasn't sure if they were marked, and no one would take the Rolex or the Audamar Piguets without the paperwork. I called Lito, and he said he knew some people in St. Martin that would be able to take the diamonds off of my hands. As far as the Rolexes and the other jewelry, he said I could easily get rid of them in the Bahamas or Turks and Caicos. After speaking with Lito, I decided to go back into the room and fill my niggas in on how we could cash out on the bling!

I looked at Monsta and couldn't deny that he was one hell of a nigga because they fucked bro up bad. Money and company had killed his moms, his best friend, have him sneaking around the city, kidnapped his bitch, and now he is sitting here with a fractured wrist, a busted lip, swollen cheekbone, and a dislocated shoulder. Yet, the only thing I see in his eyes when I look at him is determination. I filled them in on what my mans told me and they were down. I went into my room got my Mac out of my Fendi backpack, got on Expedia and got three tickets to St. Martin.

"We leave at 6:45 a.m."

"Nigga, that's in three hours."

"Yea, I know."

BIG DUCKY

$\mathcal{C}$oming back from the Islands was more of a risk than actually taking the shit over there.

We profited fifty million dollars in total, and the majority of that came from the IF diamonds. The buyer advised us to place the money into one of their local banks because it was safe and untraceable and the interest rate was unheard of and hard to beat. One would think having fifty million dollars would make one's life easy, but it was a lot more complicated than you think.

With that kind of money, you just can't travel back on U.S. soil without explaining where it came from. Then if you do have a valid explanation, Uncle Sam is gone to need his percentage. Speaking of that motherfucker, how is he my uncle when clearly I'm black, and he is white. And why do I have to pay a motherfucker I can't meet in person? I look at it for what it is— mass extortion. These mother-fuckers are charging us to live.

After going over everything with the local banks, we've learned that we wouldn't be able to have access to the money until two weeks later. With everything that's going on, the entire reason for the money is to get enough of it to get what needs to be done, done!

We all agreed to give the bank half the money for safe keeping, and send whatever else we could send through Western Union and Money-Gram. We bought as many money orders we could, then went to the local casino and bought some chips, fucked around a bit, and then cashed them. Instead of taking cash, we had the casino wrote us a check each. We bought gold and a few expensive pieces to take back with us. So in all, we were able to bring twenty-three million back onto U.S. soil. We left the rest in the banks, but regardless we were now wealthy men, and I'm sure we had enough juice to get at that nigga money.

The next day we were back at where we left off getting shit together. In the process of closing on a house in Camp Creek on the south side of Atlanta, my iPhone started going off dinging and ringing all at once. I reached into my pocket, grabbed my phone, and signaled to my realtor to give me a second as I motioned to the phone. He pointed at his watch to remind me that we were fighting against time.

I swiped my thumb across my screen and picked up for the strange number that called me four times back to back.

"Hello, babe?"

"Kee-Baby?"

Her voice was like a smooth melody I couldn't get enough of. I wasn't sure why she wasn't calling me from her number, but more alarming was the fact that she was whispering and sounded like she was trying to tell me something all I heard was...

"Tell Monsta..." and then the motherfucking line went dead.

I immediately hit the number right back, but it went straight to voicemail. I tried that star sixty-seven shit, and it still went to voicemail. I tried calling her regular line, and that went to voicemail as well. I had a real bad vibe about the entire phone call the whole entire shit was way off to me. I tried to relax and not think negative, but the obvious was almost like the elephant in the room.

I hit Monsta line and told him what happened. He told me to give it some time and see if she calls back. He agreed that it was a fishy call and he himself is curious to know what she had to tell him.

I ended up staying for the closing of the house. Everything was a bit delayed when a last minute offer came in ten thousand over our asking price, and we had to double what our competition was offering in order to convince the owner of the house to move forward with us. He did, and seven hours later, we were owners of a two point two-million-dollar house.

Monsta pulled into the four-car garage in a midnight black Bugatti one of the world's fastest street cars. Taz towed behind him in an all black and chrome 2018 Ram Dually truck pulling a trailer with three black 1,400 Suzuki Hyabusas.

I never left the house because while the realtor was going over the closing and what not, I was on the phone with Brinks security. Monsta reminded me of Tony Montana when he called me and told me to spend whatever on security. I had Brinks installed their most recent and upscale security system. It came equipped with motion sensor detectors, twenty-nine hidden HD cameras with color and sound. I also had them install a solid steel gate that can stop an eighteen-wheeler traveling at a hundred miles per hour.

After another five or six hours Brinks was on their way out the driveway. Monsta and Taz waited until they were completely out of sight to unload the Dually. I assisted them, and we made about seven trips back and forth from the truck to the house.

Monsta bust the first crate open and four brand new upscale assault rifles. Sitting neatly packaged in a few of the crates, were some sub machine guns, high powered sniper rifles, lots of ammo, suppressors, C-4, dynamites, gun powder, hand grenades, and flash bombs. Top-notch bulletproof vests and clothing were in one of the crates, along with night vision goggles and binoculars. In a nutshell, we had enough artillery to start a small army, and that's exactly what the fuck we were about to do.

* * *

MY MANS TAZ had called over a few girls that worked at Onyx. The girls were some super bad porn star looking babies. I mean I understood his logic. We were about to dive head first into some deep shit and to be honest how shit has been going we were not sure if we were going to make it out, so why not live a little while we can.

By the time I went and took a shower, the entire night went left, but in a good way, I guess.

When I walked back downstairs, two bad females were taking turns sucking and slurping on Monsta's dick, while across the room three females were fucking each other. I looked on as the one with the huge ass positioned herself on all fours and arched her back. The pretty red one with the tiny tits with the piercing hungrily stuck her tongue in her asshole ramming her head viscously into her dark opening, while her chocolate athletic-built friend slammed a huge strap on into her tight little pussy. I looked on as her ass wobble with every stroke.

The moans and cries of pleasure were so intense that I think it made me overly excited to the point my dick couldn't function; it was just way too much going on. I heard a loud slapping noise and turned my attention in that direction, only to see a big booty— I mean really huge ass cheeks— bouncing out of control. As she jumped up and down on Taz, it seemed like she was jumping so fucking high and just slamming her body down on him and grinding. Someone then crept up from behind of me and started stroking my flaccid dick. After a couple of minutes of nothing happening, I must say I admired this young girl's ambition and dedication to perform and do her best to wake the dead, but I was thinking too much into it. This type of shit never happened before, so I know it's just something I'm not used to. So instead, of letting her proceed to waste her time I asked if she would like to go somewhere with a bit more privacy and she asked if we could go to the garage.

I turned on the lights, and the garage came to life exposing brand new foreign machines but the one that caught her eyes was the midnight black 2018 Bugatti.

"Oooh baby, are you fucking kidding me? Is this what I think it is?"

"What do you think it is?"

"A fucking Bugatti!!"

"It might be."

"Yo! This is crazy. Come here, come here and feel my pussy!!"

I did, and it was meaty and dripping like a faucet— literally dripping. I looked on as she walked up to the Bugatti and slowly walked around the Italian machine with admiration. With every step she took, I analyzed how her hips and ass would dance in union tantalizing me.

I immediately started to feel my ten-inch dick started to come alive against my thighs. And with every step she took, I watched her huge breasts bounce and her soft ass wobble. My dick was jumping against my inner thighs ready to stretch her little pussy out. She eventually made her way back around to the hood of the car, climbed on top of it, turned over on her back, and spread her legs so far back it made her pussy sit up like an ant bed.

"I want you to fuck me deep and hard, daddy! Please come get this pussy. Fuck me and please don't let me beg for it!" I took my dick out of my gray sweats, stroked it a few times, placed the condom on, and then positioned the helmet of my dick to her welcoming slippery hole.

Her eyes rolled to the back of her head as she bit down on her bottom lips, as I slowly pushed my manhood as deep as her tight pussy would allow me. I rotated my hips in a slow circular motion as the head of my dick massaged the bottom wall of her pussy bringing her to an instant orgasm. She exploded beneath me, and her muscles contracted on my hard dick almost forcing me out of her cunt.

As the cream from her pussy drips down my balls, I continued to slam myself deep and hard into her as she demanded loudly with every trust begging me for more. Her cries combined with the warmth and snug fit of her pussy, I couldn't contain myself any longer. As my balls slapped against her warm asshole, I felt my scrotum began to tighten, and all the blood in my body rushed to the tip of my dick. Hearing her beg me to ram my dick in her mouth and dump my load down her throat didn't make things easier for me either.

I hurriedly ripped the condom off my dick as she positioned herself face to face with my pulsating dick. She opened her mouth wide and stuck her tongue out, even flicking at the head of my dick as I rubbed only the head of my dick with my index finger. And right before I felt my nut about to bust, I grabbed her by her ponytail and stuff my rod deep into her mouth and began to pump my cum down her throat until she gagged by the overflow.

"Fuck! Did you just come home from prison? That's a lot of cum my nigga!" she said with a concerned look on her face as she wiped her mouth with the back of her hand then she giggled, kissed my dick, then ran back into the house.

Out of breath, I leaned against the Bugatti, looked back at it, and smiled devilishly, who says money doesn't buy you happiness?

MONSTA

"*J*ah! Jah! Jah! Please, I need you... Jah! Jah! Please, baby, I'm so sorry please baby heeelllpp me! JAAAAHHH!!!*"

AGHH! Fuck!

This was the second time having a dream like this. I swiped my hand over my face, wiping the beads of sweat off of my head. I looked over at the time, and it displayed *3:09 a.m.*

I remember my grandmother would always tell me that every dream ain't a dream some things we see are visions and signs.

The fact that I'm dreaming of just her voice calling out to me, and no matter where I look in the dream, and no matter how close I came to the voice, she still wasn't anywhere in sight. To be honest, a part of me wanted to think that my dream was showing that no matter how hard I look and no matter what I do, I won't be able to find the love of my life, even though her soul may be crying out to me. The thought of that alone being a possibility, caused my blood to boil, and at that point, I didn't give a fuck what I dreamed about or even what my grandmother used to say.

I know that the devil sometimes uses dreams to torment a mother-fucker and what I know as truth is mind over matter. I'm gone find Serenity, and I'm gonna make all this shit right. I was saying that to myself and to be honest, I'm not even sure if I believed myself or if I was just trying to convince myself.

Regardless of what, one thing I know for sure and two for certain more than anything, I'm ready to die defending my mother. Money has got me fucked up if he believes for a second I would ever pipe down and let him continue to live like he's the boss of all bosses, knowing he killed my mother fucking momma. That fuck nigga has got me fucked up.

I got up, took a cold shower, and was now restless, so I decided to take a drive and clear my mind a bit. I packed a sub machine gun with two .45 with extra ammo just in case history chose to repeat itself. The last time I wanted some fresh air, I ended up a hostage, and I refuse to ever get caught slipping like that ever again.

I opened the garage and then ever so lightly, pressing the gas pedal, the Bugatti bolted forward with much power that it pushed me back into the seats. I opened the main gate, took my 2.5 million dollar car out into the open, and opened her up coming down Camp Creek Parkway. As the engine growled behind me, I also noticed that I had flashing blue lights behind me coming from an unmarked vehicle. It looked like a new model Charger, and it was a red color to as well, so I know it had to be a narc or a detective.

I decided to pull the foreign machine into a dark alley. When I did, the Charger parked only a few feet away from me. Seconds later, a tall, dark-skinned nigga stepped out of the car wearing an obvious thick ass bulletproof vest. *Ole Robo cop looking ass nigga*, is all I thought to myself.

He tried shining the light into my car, but I had the windows double tinted, which I'm probably assuming is the reason why he was stopping me. He tapped his flashlight against the glass again, and I had to think quick because I didn't need this shit turning into a scene and shit. Then it hit me like a punch to the jaw. Police were always one of the M.O.B.'s most valuable pieces due to them being able to provide priceless information on snitches and whereabouts of the enemy.

"What you, one of these celebrity rappers or something?"

"Nah I'm just a regular citizen."

"Good, because if you were one of them little spoil punks, I'd be writing you the highest fucking ticket I could have written for these illegal ass tints. Wassup man, my name is Detective Chambers. I always admired these motherfuckers, and I know that's all I'm gone be doing with my salary is admiring, wishing, and dreaming. How much for this baby?"

"2.5."

"Sheeew! Shit! What do you do again, brother? Hopefully, you're hiring."

"And maybe I am. I tell you what I'm gone jump in the passenger seat and I'm gone let you take this baby for a spin, and then maybe we can go over your resume. Let's just call it an interview."

"You're fucking with me, right?"

"I'm not, get in."

I left the .45 on the floor to see if he would be on some police shit asking for paperwork and shit, and if he did, he would be the world's most unluckiest guy. To my surprise, he handed me my strap and said to never not keep it on me. I told him I agreed. He fastened his seatbelt and just like I was shocked by the power this motherfucker holds under the hood, he was too. He also was a bit frightened that I was afraid he would crash it.

I told him, "Just keep going. Eventually, you will get the hang of it."

He smiled nervously.

"Damn, this baby has a lot of power behind it. I'm scared to press the fucking gas here man!"

"Take your time; you got it. Take it on I-285."

"Are you serious?"

"Yea, go for it."

The engine howled as the horses came to life behind us. He pushed the Bugatti forward in record-breaking speed. When it fishtailed, I could tell it scared the fuck out of Detective Chambers, but when he did got it under control I reached into my glove compartment and pulled out twenty-five thousand dollars I had got back from the dealer as a token of their appreciation of me purchasing the car cash.

I handed Chambers the envelope when he got to the red light, and when he looked inside, his eyes widened.

"If you work for me, I guarantee buying one of these would become nothing to you. You would be able to do it with your eyes closed."

"What I need to do?" was the only thing he asked of me while he stared at half of his salary sitting in his lap. I encouraged him by stating the obvious.

"You made half of your years' salary in less than fifteen minutes doing less work than what the pigs want you to do. All I ask of you is that you provide me with the intel I ask for and keep me ten steps ahead of them devils, can you handle that?"

"Fuck yea! What kind of question is that? Shit, I work hard in hopes of getting rich. Fuck the police, do you understand me?"

"Yea I hear you, but I need you to do something for me, and I need it done as soon as possible!"

"What's that, my man?"

I need you to tell me where I can find Dinero "Money" Moorehead. Give me a list of places he sleeps, eats, shops, and shit like that, do you understand?"

"I'm on top of it, and that shouldn't be hard because I actually overheard that we are not to fuck with him under no circumstances because the C.I.A. was on his trail, and anyone who has intelligence interested in them can be a bit difficult to tail and shit. I would advise you walk light with this one."

"Man, fuck all of that! Give me what I ask for and we're good. I'll give you another twenty-five when everything checks out."

Chambers pulled my Bugatti back into the dark alley he pulled it out of, thanked me for the opportunity, and assured me he would be in touch shortly with the intel I asked for and maybe more.

I was impressed by how smooth things ran with Chambers. Running into him was a blessing all in itself because information is power and if it wasn't for the paper, he would have been a hater. Instead, he wants to be on the team because I don't give a fuck who you are everybody wants to be a part of the winning team— everybody in America wants some money, quick money.

So with that being said, I made my way back to the nest because the name of the game right now is patience. I couldn't wait to get back and let them boys know what the fuck just happened. The bottom line is now that I got my paper up I can go toe to toe and pound for pound with Money's pussy ass. I made a vow to my moms that I would revenge her death and I know she wouldn't rest until I put that fuck nigga right next to her, and on top of that, I know Serenity loves me, and a part of me knows she needs me. As God is my witness, I won't stop until I get her back. I refuse to lose to this fuck nigga one more time, and whoever this Chino nigga is he's in the way, and if he doesn't move over, he's gone get run the fuck over period.

KEELAH

"I'm going to ask you one more time. Who the fuck were you on the phone whispering to?"

Money was damn near choking the fuck out of me. He was choking me with so much force that he was foaming at the mouth and I was slobbing. I was regretting trying to sneak into the house to retrieve some important paperwork that I needed. The last thing on my mind was him coming home and catching me. In the midst of me grabbing all the paperwork I needed, Ducky crossed my mind. The time we spent with each other was magical. After only knowing him for a couple of weeks, I was in love with him. I don't even think it was a real love thing. I think I'm falling for him because he's showing me attention that I don't get from Money.

"Nobody!" I managed to get out before he started punching me in my face. A swift kick to the stomach sent me flying across the room.

He had knocked the wind out of me, and I struggled to catch my breath as I crawled across the floor. I looked in horror watching as he went through my phone reading messages. A mean scowl formed on his face as he unbuckled his belt.

"So you want to talk to other niggas, huh? You hate me bitch! After everything I've given your ungrateful ass! I should have put your tramp ass on the track. Since you hate me, I'm going to make sure I give you a reason to. Take all your motherfucking clothes off." He pulled the belt out of the loops and removed his gun from his waistband.

"Please Money, don't do this!" He walked over to me and yanked me off the floor. I saw my life flash before my eyes as he placed the gun to my head.

"Bitch, I'll blow your brains out in this motherfucker! Don't make me say it again. Take that shit off!" he roared.

I knew he had no problem with killing me. My ass ain't ready to die, so I slowly removed my clothes. I tremble with fear the entire time. He had the gun in one hand and the thick leather belt wrapped around his other hand. He sat his gun on the table and yanked me by my hair.

"Owwwwwwww!" I howled out in pain as he basically dragged me out of the room.

I feel like my life flashed before my eyes as he threw me into the tub. He cut the cold ass water on and started beating my wet skin with the belt. The dizzy feeling I felt from hitting my head on the tub made me feel like I would pass out. As he beat me with the belt, I drifted to another place. The pain was so much that it made me become numb.

"Please!" I mumbled.

"Shut the fuck up!" He snatched me out of the tub and starting stomping me. I was trying to cover my head, but the kicks were coming rapidly. A kick to the side of the head knocked me out cold.

* * *

"WELCOME BACK, MS. HUDSON."

I observed a lady standing over me in a white coat with a stethoscope around her neck. Looking around the room, I realized I was in the hospital. I ached with every move I tried to make. Before I could respond to her two plain clothes detectives walked in the room.

"What do you want?" I asked.

"Hello, Ms. Hudson. I'm Detective Chambers, and this is my

partner Detective Jenkins. A week ago, you were found on the side of the road naked and beaten badly. Thank goodness, a jogger found you in time, or things would have been much worse. I know you're not feeling your best, but can you tell us anything about the person who did this to you?"

"No. I don't remember anything."

I knew exactly who did this shit to me but no matter what I wasn't no rat ass bitch. I wanted nothing more than for Money to pay for what he had did to me, but jail wasn't the answer. I needed him to suffer in different ways, and I knew just what to do. I could tell that the Detective was mad at me because he knew I was lying. I didn't give a fuck though."

"So, you mean to tell me that you have no clue who did this to you?"

"Look, I told you that I had no idea who did this. Can you please leave me your card and if I remember anything I'll give you a call." He was pissed, but I didn't care.

When he handed me the card, I rolled over on their ass. Tears streamed down my face at the very thought of Money. What did I ever do to deserve this shit he done to me? This is the same motherfucker that was fucking a bitch in our home. He has no right to get mad at me when it comes down to another nigga, especially when he doesn't even want me. This shit with Monsta has turned Money into a sadistic evil son of a bitch.

"Are you in any pain, Ms. Hudson? Can I get you anything?"

"I'm fine. Can you please get me a phone I need to call someone to come pick me up?"

"Oh no! You're not in any condition to leave the hospital. A couple of your ribs are cracked, and you have a severe concussion. If you haven't noticed, you have a broken arm and wrist. I think you should just relax and try to get well.

"Thank you, but I can't stay. Please get just get me a phone!" I didn't mean to snap off at her, but I need to get the fuck out of here.

"We can't keep you against your will, but promise me that you'll take the meds I give you. If anything is wrong, please come back in." I nodded my head, yes, and she handed me the phone. Without hesitation, I dialed Big Ducky. I cried tears of joy when he answered the phone on the second ring.

* * *

FROM THE MOMENT Ducky had picked me up, he hadn't said a word to me. I didn't know if he was mad at Money or me for what he had done to me. He was now living in a condo because he decided to stay in the A longer. At this point, I was starting to regret leaving the hospital. I was in more pain then I could handle. I had to pop some Codeine pills to get comfortable and him walking around ignoring me wasn't helping one bit.

"Can you please call me an Uber?" I had been sitting in the living room on the couch, and he was in his bedroom. He had been avoiding me like the plague, and I simply couldn't take it anymore.

"Fuck you need an Uber for?" he yelled causing me to jump. That body motion made me cringe in pain. The slightest move hurt. Hell, it even hurt to breathe.

"I feel like I shouldn't have called you. Since you picked me up, you've been treating like I did something to you. I apologize for bothering you, but I didn't know who else to call."

I quickly wiped the tears that had formed in my eyes. I hated how fucking weak I had become behind Money. Here I was acting like this was my man, but Ducky didn't owe me anything. For all I know, we were just a fuck. Being vulnerable to a man was some weak bitch shit. There is no way Ducky will ever see me as being more than some bitch who gets her ass whooped. Feeling like I had embarrassed myself enough, I slowly walked away from the door.

"Man, look, I have a lot of shit going on. It's not that I don't want to be bothered. I just have a hard time looking at you like that. I want to lay hands on that bitch ass nigga, but he has disappeared. We're on his ass though."

"I can help you find him." I was taken aback by him nodding his head no to what I had said.

"Let me stop you right there. In no way shape, form, or fashion will I ever allow you to do that. If you're going to fuck with me, I have to be able to trust you. If you're willing to set him up, you might do the same to me. I'm a real ass nigga, and real niggas do real things. I will never be the type of nigga that sets another nigga up through his bitch. I got that nigga don't you worry, and I promise he'll never fuck with you again. I want you to stay here as long as you need to. Do you need me to get you anything? I need to meet up with Jah and handle some shit."

"No. I popped some Codeine because this pain is unbearable, so I just want some sleep." He gently grabbed me by my hand and walked me back to the bedroom.

"Get you some rest. I'll grab you some Witch Hazel and Epsom Salt to help take some of the swelling and the soreness away. Call me if you need me." He kissed me on the forehead and left.

I crawled in the bed and stared at the ceiling. There was a something special about Ducky. I couldn't believe he didn't want me to help them get Money. That shit spoke volumes to me. He wasn't the typical nigga that would jump at the opportunity to off their enemy.

My thoughts drifted to Serenity. I wondered how she was doing. I feel like she's in the predicament she's in because of me. I should never have lied to her. She's been my only friend through all of this shit with her father. Serenity is a sweet girl, and she deserves better than to have a sadistic ass father. Money has always claimed to love Serenity so much but uses her as a pawn in his sick little game.

My fear of Money made me betray he trust. There's a good chance that she will never forgive me. As soon as I heal up and become well enough to get around, I'm going to see her. I swear I don't care if she curses me out and calls me all types of bitches. I'll stand in the paint and accept whatever she dishes out because I deserve it. She deserves better than to be held up in that house with Chino. He and Money are the best of friends because they are alike. Birds of a feather definitely flock together. I just know that they're cooking up some type of scream. Money only befriends people that he can use for his own personal gain.

Before the meds started to kick in fully, I prayed so hard to God. I silently asked him to cover me and guide me in the right direction. I had lost my way because I allowed myself to become a victim in Money's treacherous web of deceit. I was young back when he made me fall in love with his charm. Now that I'm older, I see him for who he really is. The crazy part about it is that I no longer love him. His money and the way he spoiled me played a big part in me loving him. The little part of me that did love him slowly subsided each time he put his hands on me. After praying, my anger set in. Ducky didn't want me to help him set him up, but that didn't mean I couldn't get him back for fucking up my life. This man has snatched my soul, and it's only right I snatch his. The world would be a much better place without him in it.

SERENITY

J was in a daze as I stared out of the bedroom window at my son. He was playing basketball in the yard with Chino. His smile was as big as Lake Michigan. Chino was mean, but I could tell that he loved our son. Being around him showed me what I missed by giving him away. He called me momma, but it was hard forming a bond because Chino was trying to stop it. If Baby C asked me for permission to do something and I said no, Chino would turn around and tell him yes. Baby C would simply look at me and do what his father told him to do.

I couldn't be mad at him because he had only known me for a month. He had been with Chino and his mother since birth. I had been beating myself up for giving him away. At that moment, I didn't have the heart to raise him alone. Chino was going away for a long time. I was too ashamed to tell my father. At that time, I thought the world of my father and his opinion of me mattered. Keelah was the only one I trusted, and she betrayed me. I would have rather her talked me into keeping my son, instead of making me think she was giving him to a good family. I now know that God is punishing me for not appreciating the gift he gave me. Most women long to have kids while I was trying to give mines away.

To make matters worse, I'm sitting here pregnant with Jah's baby. I had paid the maid to bring me a test without Chino's knowledge. I had been so caught up with everything going on that I hadn't had a period in damn near two months. Here I am again pregnant and unsure of it. Jah has most likely moved on with his life. He's not thinking about me, and I know for a fact he's not ready to be a father — at least not to a father to a baby from me. *How could I let this shit happen again?* I asked myself. Looking out of the window, I saw that Baby C fell really hard, and Chino started yelling at him. I rushed out of the bedroom, down the stairs, and out of the front door.

"Are you okay?" I kneeled down and wiped the tears from his face.

"Get the fuck back! He's cool. You're gonna make him a pussy nigga with that shit!" He yanked me up and pushed back.

"Keep your fucking hands off of me. That's my son too. Checking on him to make sure that he's okay will not make him out to be a pussy."

"Was he your son when you tried to give him to fucking strangers?" He stepped closer to my face, and I stepped back. Since the night he raped me, I don't like him near me.

"That's not fair, Chino!"

"You know what the fuck ain't fair? The fact that you're here with me, but all you're thinking about is that bitch as nigga! You know what else ain't fair is sitting on the cell block waiting for a call or some bread from your bitch. It ain't fair that instead of you being a woman and telling me about you was pregnant by me you decided to give me fucking son away. Do you have any idea how I felt when my OG brought my son to see me, and I didn't even know that he existed? Don't stand your lying, conniving ass in front of me talking about what's not fair. Bitch, you don't have the right. Take your ass back in the house. Make that the last time you step in when I'm having father and son time. That shit is disrespectful, Serenity!" he barked.

"I don't have to take this shit!"

I ran into the house and upstairs to my bedroom. It was time I get the fuck out of here. I didn't want shit that he had given me. I hadn't asked for the shit anyway. The crazy part about all of this is I had been trying to get over the fact that Chino had raped me, just so I could be with my son. However, it had been hard to be around a man who had violated me in such a violent way. Chino has been walking around and acting like the shit never happened. It didn't help that he decided to do it while our son was in the same house.

"Where the fuck do you think you're going?"

"Get your hands off of me. I'm getting the fuck away from you."

I tried to walk past him but choke slammed me on the bed. Before I could fight back or tussle, he jammed a needle in my neck. I immediately became limp and unable to move. He looked at me with evil satisfaction as the drugs started to take control of me. I managed to look past him and see my son standing in the door way watching. That was the last thing I had seen before I blacked out.

* * *

As I looked around the room, I realized I was in complete darkness. The room was so dark that I couldn't see in front of my face. As I tried to move around, I realized two things. One, I had a damn headache from hell. Two, I was tied to the bedpost. In a panic, I begin to thrash around trying to get loose. All it did was tire me out. Chino had injected me with some shit to knock me out cold, and now I was tied up. Tears fell down the sides of my eyes and pooled in my ears. At the moment, I was feeling like Joan Crawford in that old black and white movie *What Ever Happened to Baby Jane*. This nigga was holding me against my will. This shit couldn't be life. Images of Jah flashed in my mind as I wished him here to save me.

I immediately begin to get angry with myself for even thinking about him. Thinking of him when I was at my worst moments was becoming a habit. I guess somewhere inside of my thick ass skull he could hear me calling out for him to save. He never came any of the other times, and I know for a fact he won't be coming this time either. The door slowly creaked open, and I looked up and locked eyes with my son.

"I'm scared and Daddy's gone. Can I sleep with you?" My heart beat raced as the wheels in my head started to turn. Chino hadn't left me unattended since I had been here. That explains why he has me tied up.

"Of course you can sleep with me, but first I need you to help me. Do you think you can be a big boy and untie me?" His eyes bulged, and I could tell he was scared.

"Daddy will be mad."

"No, he won't. I promise. If you untie me, I promise I'll take you down to Centennial Park. Remember I was showing those pictures of that big Ferris wheel?"

"Yeah. It looked like fun."

"It is fun, Baby C. Now go get the scissors from the knife block and remember to hold the sharp part down away from your face."

For a minute, he looked unsure, but he quickly ran out of the room. I closed my eyes and prayed that Chino didn't come home. My heart was damn near beating out of my chest waiting for my baby to come back.

"I got them."

"Okay! Now come over here and cut off the piece of cloth that's holding my arms up." One by one, Baby C cut my hands loose.

"Now go and put on a jogging suit and gym shoes. You have to be warm for the Ferris wheel." I kissed him on the jaw, and he raced out of the room.

I immediately started cutting away at the sheet he had tied my feet together with. Once I was free, I jumped up and threw on jeans and a white t-shirt. After putting on a pair of gym shoes and a hoodie, I raced out of the room to find my son.

"Going somewhere!" Chino said as he sat next to our son on the bed. The gun that sat next to him made my heart beat race.

Without hesitation, I took off running. Briefly looking back, I saw him on my heels. He reached out and pushed me hard as hell making me fall. He quickly dived on top of my back. I struggled with his ass because he was trying to bash my face into the floor. Somehow, I managed to flip over on my back, and he started to rain down blows on me. I was trying my best to block the punches, but his ass was making them land.

"Ahhhhh! Get off of me!" I cried.

The next couple of minutes was like things went into slow motion. The sound of a gun going off caused both of us to stiffen up. Seconds later, he fell on top of me hard as hell. I panicked and pushed him off of me. Only to be met with my son holding the smoking gun. He had shot him in the back. Chino was still moving a little, so I quickly jumped up and went over to Baby C.

"Give me the gun, baby! Now go downstairs and wait for me." I kissed him and wiped his face.

"Call the ambulance!" Blood poured out the side of his mouth as he begged for his life.

I walked into the room and grabbed a pillow. When I came back into the hallway, he was trying to scoot towards the stairs. I don't know what had come over me, but I felt a level of satisfaction knowing that he was most likely dying or paralyzed. Either way, he didn't deserve to breathe the same air I did. I placed the pillow on him and squeezed twice sending two into the back of his head. The adrenaline rush I felt pulling the trigger was something I had never felt before. Reality quickly set in, and I knew that I had to get the hell out of there. I placed the gun in my hoodie pocket, rushed down the stairs, grabbed my son, and got the fuck out of dodge.

Once I was inside one of his many cars, I didn't know where I was going to go. I knew for a fact I wasn't going to my father's house. I drove away with the intentions to get on the highway with my son and never look back. However, I found myself on the highway headed towards Jah's condo in Buckhead. Before I left Atlanta and started a new life, I needed some closure. There was no way I can go on with the rest of life and never know why he abandoned me. I needed to know why he interrupted my soul if he had no good intentions for me. I deserved an explanation as to why he never rescued me. My ass shouldn't even care what his reasons are, but I simply can't move on without the proper closure I need to remove him from my heart. Love makes you do some crazy shit. Here it is I'm trying to get closure from a nigga and just committed a damn murder.

"Did I hurt my daddy?" Baby C brought me out of my thoughts.

"No baby! You just made him go to sleep for a little while. He's just fine." I wiped my tears and continued to drive towards Jah house.

The more I drove thoughts of my father crossed my mind. I didn't understand how all of my life he was a loving father and then he turned so hateful. It made me wonder if all the things my mother used to say was true. My mother was mean as fuck, but she was adamant that my father wasn't the nice guy in the whole situation.

Thinking of my parents made me feel like I needed some type of explanation from him. How could he basically trick me to stay at Chino's house? Why would he put me in such a dangerous situation? Not to mention being in a war with Jah. From the moment he found out about my relationship with Jah, he became hateful towards me. I've always thought he was the best father in the world. I would brag on my father to every and anyone that would listen. Now, the very thought of him makes me cringe on all levels. Hate is such a strong word to use for someone who gave you life, but I hate my father. Going to confront Jah was pushed to the back of my head as I made a U-turn and went to see my father.

MONEY

"*A*re you sure that bitch didn't rat a nigga out?"

"I can assure you she didn't. She was adamant about not knowing who did the shit to her. I honestly think the blows to her head made her forget."

I took a long pull off of my cigar and blew the smoke in the air. That bitch Keelah had better make sure she never tells that I fucked her up. That little bitch had it coming. I should have put her ass on the stroll when her pops first dropped her ass off. She was just too fucking pretty to share with other niggas. Just thinking of all the sacrifices I made for Serenity, I should have put her ass on the stroll too.

Serenity and Keelah are some disloyal, ungrateful, unappreciative ass bitches. It was one thing for Serenity to fuck with my enemy, but another for my bitch to be fucking one of his partners. After doing some digging, I found out who the nigga was she had fucking. He's as good as dead as the nigga Monsta. I had become so deep in thought that I forgot Detective Chambers was in my office with me.

"That bitch ain't crazy. What about the nigga Monsta? Chambers, I need you to get as close to the nigga as you can. I pay you top money to fix situations for me. This Monsta situation needs to be handled immediately.

"I got you, boss man. He doesn't suspect a thing. I actually have to go and link up with him now. I might have a location on where and when his shipments come in."

"As soon as you find that shit out, I want you to blow that nigga brains. I wanted to be the one to kill that nigga myself, but he doesn't have to breathe any longer than what he already has. I need that motherfucker dead, so I get back to this money. This bloodshed on the street has got my fiends scared to come out and get the product. This young street punk is burning shit down and murking motherfuckers if he sees them buy from my youngins. I've lost damn near forty percent of my street team. Either he's killed them, or they're too fucking scared to work while he's on the damn loose. His mammy should have named his ass Animal instead of Monsta because that's exactly what the fuck he is— an animal that needs to be shot dead. Humans do act the way this motherfucker do. He's a vicious ass creep. Out here killing niggas and dismembering them. That's some Jeffery Dahmer type of shit."

Just thinking about this motherfucker, Monsta had me mad as fuck. In all of my years of running these Atlanta streets, I never had a nigga who was a problem. This nigga Monsta is like a painful boil on my ass that wouldn't go away.

"Calm down, Boss! I got him. Let me head out and meet up with him. I'll keep you in the loop while I'm out with him." Chambers and I dapped it up, and he left to meet up with the nigga Monsta.

The sound of my alarm system beeping made me grab my Glock from my desk drawer. As soon as I made it to the foyer, I quickly put it away. Serenity and Baby C were standing there.

"What are you doing here? Where's Chino?"

"Fuck Chino! I'm here because I want to know what I ever did to you besides fall for the wrong man."

"I'm not about to have this discussion in front of my grandson. As a matter of fact, I'm not about to have this conversation with you. You made your choice, and now I'm making mines. Get out of my home!"

"What choice did you give me? From the jump, you made this thing about you. This is deeper than me having feelings for Jah. At what point did you think it was cool to interfere with my decisions? How could you call yourself a father and you walked around knowing my son was being raised by Chino. He could have been with a good caring legit family. His grandfather and his father are drug dealers. I didn't want this for him. You had no right to go against my wishes, Daddy!" Serenity was crying, and it didn't faze me because I knew it was all fake.

"I'm Dinero "Money" Moorehead, and I do whatever the fuck I want. You're standing here crying because I didn't let you give my fucking grandson to some damn strangers. That's weak shit. Don't stand right here judging me about my parenting. Your disloyal ass has only been a mother for about a month."

"I'd rather be the best thing that happened to him in a month than the worst thing that happened in his life. You've spent my whole life claiming to be the best father in the world. All of that shit was a façade. There is no way you could have ever loved me. I'm starting to think you aren't my father because a real father would never treat his child like this."

"Your momma was my bottom bitch that broke bad. I'm quite sure I'm not your real father. However, it was my obligation to take you away from her junkie ass and give you a better life, which I did, only for you to turn out just like her deceitful ass."

I never meant to reveal that I probably wasn't her father like this. It was something I vowed to take to my grave. At this point, there was no need to take it back or try to sugar coat it. Her bitch ass momma was a whore that did dicks for a living. Now don't get me wrong I chose to take on the responsibility, but the bitch got strung out. That's when I decided to try and get Serenity. When the bitch died, I decided to raise her up as my own because they had no other family who wanted Serenity. As far as I'm concerned, she should be thankful her ass didn't become a ward of the state.

"I'm happy to know to that you aren't my father. You don't deserve the title. Have a nice life. I'm sure it won't last long at the rate you're going. You're an evil ass man, and you belong in the pits of hell with the Devil."

"I'll make sure to greet your nigga Monsta when I get there. I guarantee you he'll be there before me."

I hated to be so cold, but it's her own fault for pushing me to this point. I walked away from her and back into my office. The sound of the door slamming outside let me know that she was gone. Before I could rest good, I received a text from Chambers letting me know he had the information and he was getting ready to head over to Monsta's crib and handle him. I definitely wanted in on that. I suited up, called some of my goons, and headed over to off his bitch ass once and for all.

MONSTA

I had been watching my nigga cater to Keelah, and I knew he was feeling her. He was a dog out here in these streets, so to see him fucking with one woman heavy was new to me. It also made me miss Serenity even more. It was like my street life interfered with having a good life with her. I was still trying to process the shit her pops told me. I didn't want to believe she had a long lost kid and a nigga. One of the things that attracted me to her was the fact that she didn't have kids already. I wanted to be the first to give her that.

It's obvious she had been keeping secrets from a nigga. I'm not mad at her because the shit was before my time. However, I think she should have told me about it. Then again she doesn't seem like the type of girl who would abandon her child.

Besides my mind being consumed with thoughts of Serenity, I've been beating these motherfucking streets up. A nigga has been murking every motherfucking thing in sight that's standing in my way. I literally hadn't had a moment's peace or sleep within the last couple of months. Fucking with this nigga Money had been more than I bargained for but very lucrative. I've damn near depleted his fucking existence in these streets. We've taken his blocks and damn near all of his clientele. It was a blessing to have my niggas Taz and

Big Ducky with me. We were out straight killing shit with no fucks given. Snatching lives is right up my alley, but I'm in need of some fucking rest.

I think I need to physically rest so that I can get together mentally. This shit with Serenity had me fucked up on a personal level. On the one hand I want to find her and wife her the fuck up, but on the other hand, I want to wash my hands with the situation. It's obvious she ain't checking for the kid if she's playing house these days. Monsta doesn't chase shit, but a check and that's real.

* * *

"WHAT THE FUCK are you doing in my house?" I almost shot this bitch Lu-Lu. I had fucked with this hoe a couple of times, and I regret that shit. I have a real life fatal attraction on my hand.

"I needed to see you, Monsta. I miss you so much. You haven't been returning any of my phone calls." I looked at this bitch laid out in bed naked as the day she was born. If I didn't feel like cleaning up blood or disposing of a body, I would murk this bitch.

"Did it ever dawn on you that I don't like your bird ass? It was a fuck. That's it. That's all. Get dressed and get the fuck out my crib before I murk your bitch ass. Make this the last time you ever do some shit like this."

"I'm sorry. I've just been missing you."

I just shook my head at this bitch because she was delusional as fuck. This is what I get for fucking with a bitch based on her fat ass and her pretty face. This hoe was nutty as fuck, and I should have known it from the jump. She was sprung after spending one night with me, not to mention the fact that we had just met.

"Get dressed so you can leave my fucking house. I will not ask you again." I pulled my gun out and held it down to my side.

She needed to know that I was not fucking playing with her. This also told me that I needed to get rid of this fucking condo. The shit was too fucking accessible. She quickly jumped from the bed and started getting dressed. She was talking some shit under her breath, but I didn't give a fuck. Her ass needed to get gone. I was tired and wanted to lay the fuck down.

As soon as she was fully dressed, I snatched her ass up by the shirt and escorted her ass out.

"Damn! You don't have to do all of that. I'm leaving." She tried to jerk away but held my grip firm. I was praying I broke her fucking arm in the process. Crazy ass bitch.

When I opened the door, I was shocked to see Serenity standing there. I also took notice to the little boy's hand that she was holding. He favored her, so I knew he had to be hers.

"Who the fuck is this bitch? Is this why you're putting me out, Monsta?" Before I knew it, I had grabbed that bitch and forcefully pushed her ass out. Damn near knocking Serenity over in the process.

"Get the fuck out of here before I put some hot shit in you." I had lost all my cool as I pressed the gun to her head." She quickly yanked away from me and ran down the hall.

"I'm sorry you had to see that. Please, Serenity come inside."

"No! Money was right. You never loved me. It was all a part of your plan to get at him."

"Come on now! You know that's not true. He told you that shit to get in your head!" I walked towards her, but she stepped back.

"You never came for me. Do you have any idea what I've been through? I've been beaten, and I've been raped. I prayed that you would rescue me. Thoughts of you kept me going. What we meant to one another kept me going, but obviously, I meant nothing to you at all. While I was suffering, you were out fucking bitches. I hate your guts Jah, and I wish I never met you." She was crying, and that was causing her son to get upset. It was fucking me up seeing her all fucked up and emotional.

"Listen to me Sere—" Before I could finish the sentence, gunfire erupted all around the room.

"Ahhhhhhh!" Serenity screamed, and I watched her get hit.

As I tried to go over to her, I was hit a couple of times as well. I belly crawled across the floor to her. The condo was being riddled with bullets and shit was breaking all around us. She was conscious but hit pretty badly.

"Just breathe, everything will be okay," I managed to say but wasn't so sure. I had some serious wounds, and so did she.

"My baby," she said in a strained voice.

It was then I remembered her son. I looked on the side of her and closed my eyes. I couldn't bear the sight in front of me. He had a gaping wound to his neck and was dead. Serenity started to cry and wail. I managed to crawl closer to her in an effort to comfort her. Before passing out, I vowed to get revenge for Serenity and her lil' man if God saw fit for me to beat this shit. This shit had become bigger than money and territory. This shit was personal.

TO BE CONTINUED!!!!!!

TO BE CONTINUED!!!!!!

CPSIA information can be obtained
at www.ICGtesting.com
Printed in the USA
LVHW03s1242230818
587441LV00002B/228/P

9 781974 192892